The story so far, of the five from *Urban Heroes*.

Gavin – has been three years with London Albion Youth Team and is now an established reserve-team player. Ambition: to make the first team and become a fully-fledged Irish international.

Hammer – (real name Shane) is also with London Albion. He's on a short-term yearly contract and his prospects seem to be limited to the reserves. But he's a tryer. Won't give up without a struggle.

Elaine – is in Italy, establishing herself as a soccer star with Juventus Ladies in Turin. It's tough going. New country, new language, new football style. But she's determined to stick it out.

Jake – is doing his utmost to turn his band, Scorpion Jack, into a big-name draw.

Luke – is looking for a job that will, hopefully, enable him to combine earning a living with his real love in life – pigeon-racing.

Young Champions is the story of how they all make out …

PETER REGAN writes from personal experience. He once managed a schoolboy team and as 'Chick' Regan masterminded the Avon Glens and Brighton Celtic. Today he is a spectator, following the fortunes of Liverpool and Glasgow Celtic.

Young Champions is the third in his soccer trilogy – the others are *Urban Heroes* and *Teen Glory*. Also by Peter Regan: *Touchstone, Revenge of the Wizards*.

Peter Regan
YOUNG CHAMPIONS

Illustrated by Terry Myler

CHAMPION PRESS

To
Maura Wyse Tormey
– with thanks

*All characters are fictional.
Any resemblance to real persons, living or dead,
is purely coincidental.*

First published 1995 by
Champion Press
an imprint of Anvil Books
45 Palmerston Road, Dublin 6
Reprinted 1997, 2003

ISBN 0 947962 92 1

Typeset by Computertype Limited
Printed by Colour Books Limited

1

London Albion's reserves were mainly composed of a mix of young and older professionals, a few fringe first-team players and others fighting their way back on to the first team after a period of being injured – or dropped. They had a completely different management team and coaching staff from the Youths and the first team and played in the South East Counties League.

Gavin and Hammer were teamed up with Mick Bates and Cyril Stevens from their Youth-team days. Hammer played at the centre of the defence with Cyril Stevens, who had reverted back to the centre-half position after a spell of playing centre-forward during his last season at Youth level. Mick Bates, as usual, was playing his customary robust role anchoring the London Albion midfield. Gavin played more of a free role in midfield. He operated in the wide spaces, free of markers, and his wily midfield generals only played the ball to him when he had plenty of room to move in, plenty of room to use his speed and tight ball control.

Gavin and Hammer learned fast with the reserves, faster than with the Youth team. Playing with the reserves was much more practical and the players were given their heads. With the Youth team the coaches had been too overpowering; everything had to be done to their rule, else a chap would suffer the indignity of getting bawled out in front of the other players. The reserves were never bawled out; there were too many old-timers and the coaches seemed to be afraid of them. Gavin and Hammer soon realised that there was a lot to learn about professional football, and a fair share of it had very little to do with ball-playing.

Dwight Crawford was four years older than Gavin and already had some first-team experience. He was a midfield player with great potential, and it was a certainty he would one day play for England. Something of an eccentric, he suffered from a gigantic ego; he had a great belief in his own ability and thought he was the best player at the club. And it was usually in an attempt to bring him back down to earth that he was dropped to the reserves.

The reserves had a nickname for him: 'The Informer'. They always had a bit of a lark after away games and Dwight had a habit of bringing stories back to John Warner, the first-team manager, about what went on. He was getting a lot of players into trouble. The occasion for a lesson came when he was listed to play for them in a nice little outing against Brighton.

After the match the players had their usual shower. But they left the showers quickly, grabbed their clothes – and those of the 'informer' – and left him, stitchless, locked up in the shower area. They didn't hang around the grounds; they got into the team coach and drove up the motorway towards London. When they arrived, Dwight Crawford, wearing the opposition's rig-out, club blazer and all, was there ahead of them, he had got a taxi and put it down on the club's expense-sheet.

'Never knew you got a transfer, mate,' chirruped Mick Bates. 'I thought transfers didn't come through tha' quick.'

'You haven't heard the end of this,' fumed Dwight Crawford.

And they hadn't. John Warner was hopping mad. But they got off. The 'informer' didn't get off so lightly, though. He was fined, and told off for taking the liberty of putting the taxi trip back to London down to the club's expenses.

But it all ended well. The team chipped in and paid the fine. The 'informer', in appreciation, didn't inform any more, and from then on any indiscretion never reached

John Warner's ears. Nor was Dwight in the habit of dallying in the showers on away games again. A quick plunge and then out. He was always sitting in the coach well before the others left the dressing-rooms. He went on to play Premiership football for years. and to play for England. But he never lost his aversion to showers.

Both Gavin and Hammer knew it wasn't going to be a great season for London Albion's reserves. But they, like Mick Bates, Cyril Stevens and Dwight Crawford were young and enthusiastic. Unlike the older pros, they saw their futures still before them, as yet unspoilt by failure, rejection or injury. Unlike some on the reserves, their progress was on an upward curve. To maintain and improve their current form would take more than just sweat and tears. It would take character and staying-power to bridge the gulf and secure a place on the first-team squad. If they were to come through they would owe a lot to Bill Thornbull, their ex-Youth team trainer. Maybe Bill honed fitness, but he steeled character.

'You play with your feet. But the difference between winnin' an' losin' comes from inside your head.' That was philosophy.

Winning and losing was what professional football was all about.

And who wanted to be a loser?

Nobody. Bill Thornbull's words haunted many a player:

'It's not you the club wants, son. It's the ability you have. Lose that an' the club won't be long in showing you the door. An' probably the back door at that.'

Sad fact – sad sport.

Two weeks later Gavin and Hammer received a phone-call at London Albion's training-ground at Highfield. The call was from Jake in Greystones.

'I rang your digs, The landlady said you were movin' into a new house.'

'Yeah, I put a payment down on a house,' replied

Gavin. 'The Boss says the responsibility will do me good. Might give me the courage to get married.'

'You're not gettin' married? You haven't blown a fuse, have ye?'

'No. Anyway, buyin' a house is a good investment. It's better than money in the bank.'

'What's Hammer goin' to do?'

'He's movin' in with me.'

'I hope that's an open invitation.'

'What do you mean?'

'Well, if I'm ever over in London, I could stay there too.'

'Fair enough, once you don't bring you mad band over.'

'We're not that mad. We've gone professional. At least we're not like Luke and the others we went to school with. At least we've got jobs.'

'What's Luke doin'?'

'Just him and his pigeons. He was on a FÁS course, but it came to nothin'. I think he was makin' wooden legs for tables.'

'You're jokin'?'

'No, I'm not. There's nothin' doin' over here. Only for the band I'd have no job. So much for school and an education.'

Sad to say most of the lads Jake had gone to school with weren't academically minded. Prior to their sitting for the Leaving Certificate, two ex-team mates from Gavin and Hammer's Shamrock Boys days, Gummy Davis and Rasher Murphy, were totally washed-up. The Leaving Cert really got to them. Gummy was on twenty cigarettes a day, while Rasher had taken to drinking washing-up liquid in the hope he'd catch a mysterious stomach bug and be rushed to hospital. But nothing happened, except that he began to blow bubbles now and again. God had endowed him with a marvellous constitution. A pity He didn't do anything for his brain.

'How's Lar Holmes doin' with his football team?'

'Well, they're still in the Dublin Schoolboys. Them and

Riverside. Though there's talk of Riverside gettin' thrown out. They're back in the People's Park. Chopper Doyle's got horses down there. The place is in an awful state. Everybody – but everybody is givin' out. Riverside'll get kicked out all right.'

'Are you still giving Lar a hand with his team?'

'No. Like I told you, me and Scorpion Jack are gone professional. I haven't got the time?'

'The club scene must be going well, then.'

'It is. We hope to cut a demo-tape soon.'

'What for?'

'To send to England, of course. Hopefully we'll attract one of the big record companies. It'll be all our own material. Songs me and Dave wrote. If you aren't in you can't win, How's it goin' for you and Hammer?'

'Not bad. Maybe a bit better for me than him. It'll work out.'

'I envy you. I always wanted to be a footballer. Only thing, I was brutal.'

'It didn't stop you from being a classy guitar player. Where are you ringing from?'

'The phone-box at Blacklion. The thing's gone mad. I got through for twenty pence. Everyone's here. It's the best value in town.'

'How's Elaine doing in Italy?'

'Haven't heard. Elaine was always too posh for the likes of us. Saw her Da the other day. Elaine'll make out all right. She's got brains. Listen, I'd better go. There's a Japanese fella outside the phone-box making faces. I think he wants to ring Tokyo. See you.'

Jake hung up.

Gavin tucked in his track-suit bottoms and went outside to join the rest of the reserves for training.

It wasn't all plain sailing for Elaine. Not only was the Italian style of football difficult to adjust to; there was something of a culture shock as well, the language being a big problem. The going was tough, all the more so because the Italian mentality wasn't overtolerant; they expected their players to be in top form all the time – and Elaine's suffered in the early days while she struggled to come to terms with her new surroundings. Six indifferent games and the fans weren't exactly over the moon about her. But she was determined not to allow her poor start to her Italian career to get her down. It was probably the club's fault for selecting her on the first team so quickly. Maybe it would have been better to edge her in gradually with an adjustment period on the reserves.

The manager, Dariusz Kowalczyx, was Polish. As a player, he played for GKS Katowice and Legia Warsaw. His name, along with those of the Italians, Yugoslavs and Belgians of the Juventus squad, added to the alienation and strangeness Elaine felt at first.

After her sixth game in the Serie A, Elaine asked to be dropped from the first team. Her confidence was beginning to suffer. It was bad enough to lose form, but to lose confidence would be a total disaster. She had a quiet word with Dariusz, who saw the danger signals and allowed her to step down to reserve-team football. There the going was a lot easier, the standard less demanding.

Playing with the reserves may have been dull, unglamorous and dreary, not much better than park football really, but those three months gave her a chance to find her bearings. There was plenty of time out of the limelight to learn the language and get used to the Italian way of life. She began to settle, made friends and found that Turin had a sense of home about it. It wasn't such a strange place after all.

At the end of her time on the reserves she was called on to join the first team for a league fixture away to Lazio. Juventus won 1-2. Elaine played fairly well. She felt comfortable and worked up a good understanding with her fellow players.

The following week they were at home to Firenze from Florence. Elaine played the full game and had a hand in one of the goals scored. Dariusz Kowalczyk was pleased with her form; he could see a marked improvement. She was given extra time with her coaches to make her more aware of what they expected from her tactically and, as her Italian was picking up, most of what they were saying registered. The first-team players were beginning to respect her. They could see that she was going to turn out something special. Within a year, or two, she would set the Serie A alight. She was their own 'Chichi'.

A blue and yellow Wicklow County Council truck drove slowly along Bray's Lower Dargle Road. The truck had just left the maze of small auxiliary side streets that ran adjacent to the Dargle River. The crew of three were on the look-out for a reported broken water-pipe. It was early autumn and the leaves from the massive line of trees that flanked one side of the People's Park were scattered both inside and outside the park's railings in a brown and golden yellow carpet.

The truck circled the Lower Dargle Road area for half-an-hour but failed to locate the reported water burst. Finally it pulled into the small slip road at the west end of the Park and the crew prepared to brew up. From under a pile of wet gear one man produced a gas-ring and very soon three happy men were enjoying a mug of tea each. They had come to the conclusion that the burst-pipe call was a bogus one, thought up by some of the children who lived in the vicinity of the Park, namely some of the boys who played soccer for Riverside Boys, the local schoolboy soccer club. They were probably lying low in some nearby laneway or garden, or across the Dargle River which bordered the far side of the Park, having a smoke and a good snigger.

The County Council crew were from the Greystones-Killincarrig area. Regardless of where they were working, they had their regular hideaways, and liked nothing better than plenty of tea and a chat, usually about football. The three crew members were Sean Dunlop, Eddie Reilly and Lar Holmes, newly promoted from the 'Cut the Grass Division'. Lar Holmes would be familiar to some; to others he was just a County Council nobody.

They all loved soccer and were involved in the game at one level or another, Sean and Eddie at junior level and Lar with schoolboys. In fact, Lar Holmes had been Gavin and Hammer's first ever football manager, when they had played as Shamrock Boys out of the Railway Field in Greystones. Presently Lar was managing an U-14 team for Shamrock Boys in the Dublin Schoolboys League. Riverside Boys were also involved. Hence the bogus call to the Lower Dargle Road. Riverside were always up to some kind of devilment when they knew Lar's Council truck was on call around the Bray area. For Lar, working in Bray was like being in Indian Territory. Lar was the US Cavalry; Riverside the Apaches.

Lar was very proud of the fact that Gavin and Hammer had started their football careers under his tutelage. Only the previous week they had been over in Ireland playing for the Irish U-21 team in a European Championship qualifying game, a match they had won 1–Nil against Norway. Lar had organized a minibus and brought his entire U-14 squad to the game in Tolka Park.

That was last week. Now it was the People's Park in Bray, sitting parked in the slip road having a mug of warm tea with his workmates. Lar had a photograph of the U-21 team that had played against Norway, plus the match programme on show in the cab.

'Great match! Great lads Gavin and Hammer. Never gave me an ounce of trouble all the years they played for me.'

'Fair play. You had some good ones over the years.'

'Good ones yeah, loads. But nothin' as good as Gavin and Hammer.'

'You had that Elaine Clarke too. The girl that's playin' in Italy.'

'Great kid. She gave a dig-out with my U-14s when they were U-12s. Her and Jake Flynn.'

'He's the lad that has the band?'

'Yeah, Scorpion Jack. Mad as a March hare. Hey, see down by that wall there?'

'Where?'

'That's not one of those Riverside Comanches havin' a peek, is it?'

'Naw, it's a bush.'

'I mean *in* the bush. Hidin' in the bush.'

'Naw, it's your imagination.'

'I could have sworn I saw somethin' move.'

'Jesus, you're paranoid about that Riverside shower.'

'And why shouldn't I be? They're fit to do anythin'. They'd set the truck on fire if given the chance.'

'Easy on, Lar. They're not that bad. They're only kids. High-spirited and that.'

'Bloody delinquents!'

'Cool it, Lar. Don't shout!'

'I'm not shoutin'.'

'Right, Lar. You're not shoutin'. Anyone got the time?'

'Three o'clock. Another few hours and I'm straight home. The only way you'd get blisters in this job is from sittin' down.'

The three of them sat back in the warmth of the cab, sipped their fist-sized mugs of tea, looking silently over the lengthy panorama of the People's Park. The section nearest them, including the schoolboys' soccer pitch, was cluttered with horses. They were being tended by a youth of about nineteen. Lar Holmes recognized him straight away. He was an ex-Riverside Boys player who used to play against Gavin and Hammer, and to a lesser extent Elaine, Jake and Luke, when they played under-age soccer for Shamrock Boys. The youth's name was Chopper Doyle.

13

Lar's face lit up with a smile. The sight of the dilapidated state of the soccer pitch, mainly because of the horses, gave him a really strong sense of satisfaction. Lar hated Riverside and Riverside were in trouble. They were on the verge of being removed from the Dublin and District Schoolboys League, not because of an indiscretion in particular but because they had run into trouble with the authorities at St Gerard's, where they used to play their home Dublin Schoolboys fixtures. Some of them had been in the habit of getting a little too carried away verbally. They were given to cursing on the pitch. One of St Gerard's less liberal teachers attended a game, more to hear for himself the transmission of abusive language than to see the quality of football on offer.

'Y' effin' ...'

'Slouch ears, where's y'r head?'

The teacher was less than impressed with the torrent of abuse, and the fact that some of the Riverside players were in the habit of having a smoke in public at half-time didn't go down too well either. Not the required image of St Gerard's. Riverside would have to go.

Now they were back in the People's Park. Most of the opposing teams objected to the Park.

'There's no dressing-rooms.'

'Just trees. Trees all along the touchline.'

'And there's a river.'

'Don't forget the river. And the bloody ball goin' into it all the time.'

'And there's some kid down there with a horse.'

'A horse? He has a whole bloody herd of them!'

As luck would have it, while Lar, Sean and Eddie were enjoying their mugs of tea an official from the Dublin Schoolboys League arrived to assess the Park – Lar recognized him straight off from attending League meetings. Immediately they got out of the cab; they wanted to hear what was going on first hand because it was obvious there was going to be a confrontation between the man from the League and Chopper Doyle. Luckily the League official hadn't a clue who Lar was; the League was too big an organization for officials to know every individual team manager.

The official had a good look at the Park, particularly at Chopper's horses. There were seven nags altogether, mainly clustered around the fringes of the football pitch. The remainder were further up the Park, chewing what was on offer.

Chopper Doyle had one horse haltered with a long rope, one end of which was anchored to a goal-post. He was holding the slack, pacing the horse in an arc.

'What are you doing with the horse?' asked the official.

'Not stranglin' it anyway. I'm breakin' it in.'

'Those other horses, are they yours as well?'

'Kind of.'

'What do you mean, kind of?'

'Mister, who are you? Sherlock Holmes?'

'Who gave you permission to keep those horses here?'

'I did. Mister ... Know what?'

'What?'

'I don't like you.'

The official didn't get time to answer. A green transit van had pulled up on the road outside. Two stocky men with fists like hams got out and came into the Park. They made directly to where the horse was haltered to the goal-post. Lar Holmes, for one, knew there was going to be trouble.

'Chopper, that's our horse.'

'It ain't.'

'And one of the others belongs to us too.'

'They don't, Piebald. They're all mine.'

'They're ours.'

A slagging-match started.

The official didn't want to get involved and made for the gate as quickly as he could. His report to the League would be unfavourable. In his estimation the People's

15

Park wasn't suitable for Dublin Schoolboys football. He looked back over his shoulder. Chopper was holding his nose. Blood was splattered all over his shirt. The two men were leading the roped horse, and a mare, out of the Park on to the roadway. Quite definitely, as far as the official was concerned, Riverside would not be allowed to use the People's Park as their home venue in the Dublin and District Schoolboys League. In future if they wanted to do that they could join some other league.

Lar Holmes was delighted with the prospect. Barred from the Dublin League, Riverside's U-14 could be on the verge of breaking up. There was no league at their age-group in County Wicklow, and they'd hardly play U-15, Lar was acutely aware of the sweet pleasantness of life without Riverside. He climbed back into the Council truck. At that particular moment in time he was one very happy person.

But not for long.

As soon as he sat down there was a squashing sound, and then a very unpleasant smell. He had sat on half-a-dozen rotten eggs. Two heads looked over a garden wall beside the slip road – two of Riverside's U-14s. They were grinning from ear to ear. They vaulted over the garden wall, gave Lar the two-fingers and scarpered hell-for-leather across the road into a lane that led to the sanctuary of the side streets.

'Riverside!'

'Riverside!'

'There's only one team in Ireland!'

'R-i-v-e-r-s-i-d-e!'

Riverside had struck again. And nobody, absolutely nobody, was going to keep them out of football. Not Lar Holmes. Not the Dublin Schoolboys League. They were a resolute, if rowdy, lot. They believed they were invincible.

2

Luke Doyle had one interest in life, and that was pigeons.
Pigeons were in his blood. They dominated his life. To see
one of them winging the last few hundred yards to the
home loft after a gruelling race was the ultimate
experience as far as he was concerned. It was an
impossible sensation to describe. With no job prospects,
no chance of improving his lot, pigeon-racing was the
only thing that kept him from totally cracking up.

Already he was one of the top flyers in Ireland. At
seventeen he had won the most prestigious race in
the Irish pigeon-racing calender, the King's Cup. He had
sold the car he won and donated the proceeds to the
besieged Moslems of Bosnia, much to his father's disgust.
The family weren't very well-off. At least Luke could have
sold the car and kept the money for himself. But all that
was water under the bridge. There would be a lot more
water under the bridge insofar as Luke was concerned.

'Leave the child alone,' said his mother. 'The money
will do someone good.'

'Why not us?' grumbled his father.

Lately Luke had been improving his pigeon lofts, using
Arthur Irvine's (his mentor in Portadown) expertise in
setting up a stud situation for his King's Cup winner.
Already fanciers from all over Ireland were inquiring if
they could reserve a youngster off the King's Cup pigeon.
Although there wouldn't be any youngsters yet, not until
the end of January or early February.

Unfortunately, Luke suffered a set back with his
breeding plans. The loft in which his champion bird was
housed was broken into. The King's Cup winner and a
few other birds, all top class, were stolen. Birds that he

hoped to breed winners from for the Young Bird races in July-August.

Straightway he got on the phone to the secretary of the Bray Invitation Pigeon Club, and the secretaries of the North and South Road Federations.

'Nine of my pigeons have been taken, includin' the King's Cup winner.'

'Any damage to the loft?'

'None, except the door was forced open.'

'Has there been much traffic around your lofts lately?'

'Loads. All bookin' birds off the King's Cup winner.'

'Did you show them around?'

'Sure.'

'Never let anybody into your lofts unless you're certain who they are. If you want to do business put the pigeons in a show–pen and do your dealin' in the house or outside in the garden.'

'What can you do about my pigeons?'

'I'll notify all clubs. Give me the ring numbers so that they can be identified if they're traced.'

Luke read out the pigeon-ring numbers.

'Did you notify the Guards?'

'Yeah.'

'The clubs will see what they can do. If they don't show up in the next few weeks there's not much hope … By the way, get a proper alarm system for your lofts. Whoever pulled the job could come back again! See about getting that alarm.'

Luke thanked the man and hung up. They'd be back again? Whoever took the pigeons would be back again! At that moment he felt like throwing in the whole pigeon-racing scene.

He rang Mr Irvine in Portadown.

'Don't chuck it in, Luke. You'll regret it.'

'They say I'd want to get my lofts alarmed. It'd cost a fortune.'

'Luke, it may not be that expensive. I can pick up a

18

good system at the right price. Maybe I can come down some Saturday and fit it for you.'

'You can do that kind of thing?'

'Sure. I put in ten years installing alarm systems. With a bit of luck I'd pick up a system for peanuts. They'll have a job getting into your loft after I'm finished. Stick with pigeons, Luke. Everyone needs a hobby and pigeon-racing is in your blood, Did you put word out about the pigeons being stolen?'

'Yeah, everywhere.'

'All the clubs and the police?'

'Yeah.'

'Did you ring Customs?'

'What d'ya mean?'

'Customs. They can keep an eye on airports, ferry-ports. Your birds could be intended for across Channel – even up here.'

'I never thought of that. Who in Customs do I ring?'

'I'll look after that for you. I've a friend who works in Customs down in Dublin, I'll give him a ring. He'll put the word out. What are the ring numbers?'

Luke rhymed them off.

'That alarm system – I'll have it in the next month. I'll be in touch.'

'Arthur, I mightn't have the money to pay for it for a while.'

'Don't worry. I'm in no hurry. Good luck with the pigeons.'

Four days later two shady characters who were on the fringe of the pigeon-racing scene were stopped by Customs while boarding the Liverpool ferry at Dublin Docks. At the outset it was just a routine check. Luckily, one of the officers on duty was a friend of the person Mr Irvine had contacted. He opened the carrying-box containing the pigeons and checked the ring numbers against a list that had been left at the Customs desk. The numbers matched. They were Luke's pigeons – King's Cup winner and all. The Gardai were called and the two pigeon thieves were taken into custody, mumbling curses and vague threats.

Two hours later Luke received a phone-call, telling him to collect the pigeons from Store Street Garda Station.

'Are your pressing charges?' he was asked.

'Don't know.'

'You should.'

'Okay, I'm pressin'.'

He rang Arther Irvine at his home and recounted the whole story.

'You did right to press charges, Luke. Go soft and that type would take you to the cleaners. When are you going into Dublin to collect the birds?'

'Right now. I hope they're all right.'

'They will be. The boyos wouldn't get the money they're looking for if they weren't in top shape. I'll be down Saturday week with an alarm system – one of the best. Those thieves can keep away from your loft in future … I hope you're not still thinking of giving up pigeon-racing.'

'Not likely!'

Being a house-owner wasn't much fun for Gavin. Redecorating and putting the house in order cost him a fortune. A large chunk of his wage packet was swallowed up by mortgage repayments and extras. Though it was the housekeeping end of things that really got him down. Cooking was an ordeal. In the end it always came down to baked beans, tinned steak-and-kidney pies, toast and marmalade. Then there was the cleaning. Hoovering the house from top to bottom. No sooner had he finished than he'd have to start all over again.

He thought things would ease somewhat when Hammer moved in. But if anything they got worse. Hammer was on the same wavelength – they were both clueless. The only chore he found easy was the washing. Marvellous invention – the washing-machine. All he had to do was pop his soiled clothes into it and that side of life was taken care of. There was a lesson there. A dishwasher quickly followed, then a tumble-dryer, then a microwave.

Conversations were dominated by the nuts-and-bolts of household maintenance!

'The light won't go on in the hall.'

'Try a new bulb.'

'I did. The fault must be in the switch.'

'Can you fix it?'

'No. Can you?'

'Call an electrician.'

The electrician came. He found more than loose connections needed repairing and spent half the day in the house. Judging by the price he charged for the job he must have been a company director with share options to boot. And strictly no tidying up. Gavin and Hammer had to look after that. It led to a conversation:

'Let's go to night-school and do a course on house-maintenance.'

'We came over here to be footballers, not housekeepers.'

'It won't do us any harm. Give us something to do at night.'

'Right! But don't tell the lads at the club. They'd only roast us.'

So Gavin and Hammer went to night-school: every Tuesday and Thursday they would get into Gavin's flash Lancia and head off.

The other students, a mix of middle-aged housewives and young engaged couples eyed them curiously at first.

'Where do they go at night?' asked one of the senior pros at London Albion.

'They're goin' to night-school,' he was told.

'No clubbin'? No chasin' after girls?'

'No. They're doin' a course in house-maintenance.'

'What's that for? Are they taking the building industry

by storm?'

'No. Learnin' how to turn a switch on, change a bulb, important things like that.'

'Get them to come night-clubbin' with us some night. We'll show 'em what's important.'

'I asked them. They haven't time.'

'How come?'

'They're takin' an extra course, home economics.'

'What's that? How to take care of the housekeepin' money?'

'No. How to boil an egg without the water dryin' up.'

One morning when Gavin and Hammer arrived for training at Highfield, instead of training-bibs they were handed aprons. Worse followed. The week after they played West Ham in a reserve league fixture. Sam Gregson, the reserve-team manager, decided to give a Man of the Match award. Gavin won it. The award: a wooden spoon and mixing bowl.

Dwight Crawford thought up nick-names for Gavin and Hammer: Mary and Jane. They stuck for a while. That is until one day Gavin showed up for training with a stunning blonde. He left her outside in the Lancia. The lads were impressed. After training he drove off and left Hammer to find his own way home. That put a quick end to Gavin and Hammer's Mary-and-Jane tag.

Somewhere along the line the blonde disappeared.

'What's 'appened with the blonde?' asked Mick Bates. 'Gone off with the milkman?'

'No, furtherin' her modellin' career.'

'Tell's another.'

Secretly, Hammer was delighted to see the blonde was dropped. Blondes could be a threat, especially if they built up a lasting friendship. If he had learned any lesson, it was that he couldn't depend on Gavin to keep a roof over his head for too long. He'd have to save, get his own house, and not be relying on Gavin to put him up.

After all, London was full of blondes and there was no

telling when the next one would come along.

Scorpion Jack's demo-tape was now something more than a hope, thanks to Kev's father, who had a friend who had a friend who worked in a recording studio in Dublin. The band had to be on the premises at eight o'clock in the morning. Having been told it could take up to sixteen hours to make the three-track tape, they cancelled their Sunday-night gig so as to have a good rest and be in fine fettle for the recording. Jake was picked up in Greystones by Kev's father, and they added the rest of the group in Bray and Shankill on the way to the studio.

The studio was sectioned off and sound-proofed. One section was partitioned by a glass panel, and inside, facing the panel, sat a technician who tinkered with a mass of technical knobs and levers called a mixing-desk. This would mix the recording together and play it on to the demo-tape set on a separate table beside him.

The first hour was spent in setting up their equipment. Kev (rhythm guitar), Dave (base guitar) and Jake (lead guitar) were in separate cubicles, while Liam (drummer) was in another to the left of Jake. The technician had a microphone in front of him through which he was able to converse with the four lads. Jake and Dave shared vocals.

The microphones for the group were set up in a special way, six for the drums, one each for the guitarists, as well as an amplifier for each guitar. They all wore head-phones, band and technician.

The technician gave them three-quarters of an hour warm-up time. Then they had a short break before going for a 'dry-run' of the first track. Soon they were beginning to get the hang of things. Then the technician issued a few short instructions and some words of advice. He paused, and with a short intake of breath shouted, 'Go for a take.' It took three hours to get the first track to his satisfaction. First they did the track live. Then they took the vocals again on their own. Then they took the musical end of the track separately. The technician mixed the two, music and separated vocals together, using the mixing-desk. They did one last take live. He played back all the tapes and chose the the final one as the best take.

They didn't get out of the studio until one o'clock in the morning. They were exhausted and utterly sick of hearing the three tracks.

Kev's father sent the demo-tape off to London straightway. They could only hope the selected record company would be impressed and send a representative over from London to assess Scorpion Jack at a gig. If he like what he heard, Scorpion Jack would be invited over to London to discuss a recording contract.

In the meantime, Scorpion Jack carried on gigging and hoping for the best.

3

The ball scewed off the sodden surface of the training ground and stopped dead. The nearest player ran through the mud-spattered mire and side-footed it towards the net. It gathered force for about two yards, only to lose momentum and stop dead in the quagmire. The players hooked and poked until, finally, the ball skidded beneath the despairing dive of the London Albion reserve-team goalkeeper.

'We'll have more of that,' roared Clive Harding, the London Albion reserve-team coach. Clive was something of a perfectionist. And he was presently proving the point – even if it meant kicking lumps out of one another on the most saturated, muckiest section of the club's training ground at Highfield. London Albion reserves were down to play Brentford mid-week. Reports were that the Bees' home pitch was a quagmire. That the game would definitely go ahead was typical of officialdom's bulldog stubbornness.

'We'll have the ball right in the middle here.'

The ball was intended for Dwight Crawford. But Dwight didn't get to the ball first. Instead he tangled with Mick Bates's terrier-like tackle and the two of them slid through the muck, akin to an aeroplane without wheels taxiing along a runway.

Dwight ended up entangled in a bush.

'I've enough of this. It's bloody daft.'

'Where d'you think you're goin'? Get back out there.'

'Clive, nobody plays in that.'

'Correction. You will, Wednesday night. Brentford Reserves v London Albion.'

'Think you can count me out, Clive'

'Why, you got the 'flu'?

'No, pneumonia.'

'You prima donnas. If it was the first team and the television cameras there'd be no moans. Get back out there an' splash around like all the rest. Earn your money for a change.'

Reluctantly, Dwight rejoined the so-called kick-about.

Most of the players' jerseys and knicks were covered in mud. A few had their faces ducked in the stuff. Dwight hated playing on muddy pitches. By nature he prided himself on his appearance His top priority was to keep his football rig-out clean, even in the most important matches. Having his hair perfectly combed also mattered. He hated to have it tossed. For most matches he wore new boot-laces. And before first-team matches he would personally give his boots an extra shine before going out on to the pitch.

Dwight was tidiness personified. He felt uncomfortable playing football in the mud. In his eyes Clive Harding was damned stupid, putting them out on a section of water-logged training ground, splashing about in puddles and mud, all because they were due to play a match at water-logged Brentford. Sure Dwight could beat that lot blindfold. What he still hadn't fathomed, though, was what in God's name he was doing playing on the reserves. The more he thought about it the more infuriated he became. Whenever he played on the first team he always turned in a top-notch performance.

The reserves! In Dwight's eyes half of them shouldn't have been allowed next or near any football club, much less a club of London Albion's standing. Bar Gavin, Hammer, Mick Bates and Cyril Stevens they were all crap in his eyes. They were some kind of curse inflicted on the club. He had only to look to the goalkeeper to prove his point. Six foot five, and as empty as a clothes-line in a hurricane, looking as if famine was rife among the goal-keeping fraternity. He had played one game for the first team and made a total cock-up of it. What was worse, he was on a good wage. One thing was certain; by the look of him he wasn't spending any of it on food. He was great in the air, but on the ground he was like a dying swan. By the time he got the theatricals over with and down to the ball, the newspaper reporters would be jotting down the name of the goalscorer, looking over one another's shoulders to make sure they'd got the facts right. If Dwight ever had a kind word to say about the goalkeeper it was that he'd make a great wallpaper-hanger.

As for Clive Harding, having the players splashing about in muck and puddles ... in Dwight's eyes the man was a nutter. If Highfield were bone-dry he probably would have brought the fire-brigade in to flood the place, to simulate conditions at Brentford. Luckily he wasn't too influential a figure at London Albion. If he were reserve-team *manager* the mind would just boggle at what he might get up to.

Reserve-team manager? No way. That was the domain of Sam Gregson.

A year ago, Sam Gregson had steered one of the top North of England clubs to a Premiership title. The story of how he ended up managing London Albion's reserves was a real tragedy. He was involved in an under-the-counter deal involving the transfer of a star player. A posse of other Premiership clubs was chasing after the player, and to clinch the deal Sam Gregson handed over the often whispered-about 'money in a brown bag' to the player's manager at a roadside cafe. The money would guarantee that the manager would influence both the club and player to favour Sam's club in the event of the transfer going through, thus eliminating all the other interested parties.

Unfortunately for Sam, word about the deal circulated around the Premiership. A rival club decided to get their own back by ringing one of the tabloids.

'Want a good story?'

'Sure.'

'Meet me, cocktails and dinner. Europa Club. 7.30. Don't forget to bring the cheque-book.'

'Who's involved?'

'Sam Gregson.'

That was just a year ago. Sam had been at the height of his managerial powers, but the newspaper exposure rapidly reversed his standing. The FA investigated the allegations. Sam's club was in the firing-line, with Sam in the worst trouble of all. There were calls for his resignation. Further negative media coverage put him under more and more pressure, and in the end he had no option but to resign. A friend offered him a short-term job as a salesman. Sam's star was fixed low, buried almost below the horizon. Then Ted Brinsley, the London Albion chairman, rang him. Offered him a job as reserve-team manager.

'I don't know, Mr Brinsley.'

'For a person of your experience and success rate, to manage a reserve team seems something of an insult. But ...'

'It's not that, Mr Brinsley. I miss football. Just to be involved would mean everything. It's the Press. They might hound me again.'

'You'd have my word, they won't. It means a lot to have friends in the right places. And the Press just happen to be in that category.'

'You mean that?'

'Certainly. Being a reserve-team manager would keep you out of the spotlight for a while. It just might be the platform to bring you back into Premiership football.'

'What about John Warner?'

'John's contract is up at the end of the season. There's no guarantee he's going to stay with us. You'd be adequate cover if he were ever to leave.'

'What if he doesn't?'

'He's got a big workload as it is. We would be thinking in terms of joint-management, like they do on the Continent.'

'Think he'd go along with that?'

'Of course. He's progressive.'

'Give me a while to think it over.'

'Three weeks.'

Three weeks later Sam Gregson rang back and gave Ted Brinsley his reply. It was favourable. He accepted the position.

That was it. There was a new addition to the club: Sam Gregson, reserve-team manager. And what was even better, John Warner didn't mind in the least.

Ted Brinsley, apart from being chairman, was the power-broker at London Albion. He dictated club policy, advised on management, backroom staff, the lot. In all there were five directors. All were rich, successful businessmen who thought nothing of ploughing thousands of pounds into the club when need be. Apart from putting in appearances at home Premiership fixtures the directors met on a weekly basis in the mahogany-panelled boardroom deep in the bowels of Brompton's West Stand. Boardroom meetings were usually dead-pan affairs, except when Ted Brinsley got fired up. Ted was a larger than life character – who had made his money in the insurance business, head of a huge business conglomerate that had offices all over Britain. He was powerful and manipulative, demanding and ruthless.

One day he drove to Highfield and casually watched the reserves train. He showed particular interest in Gavin.

'How's the boy coming on?'

'Great.'

Ted said no more, pulled up the collar of his expensive mohair coat and watched a while longer, checked the time and drove off.

Back on the training ground Sam Gregson and his

backroom staff put the reserves through their paces. The forwards were taken aside along, with the goalkeepers, and put through a routine of shooting and running on and off the ball, the end product being plenty of shots at goal, volleyed or otherwise.

The outfield defenders were also dealt with separately. They had a session of zone marking. A few of the first-team forwards were sent over by John Warner and let loose on the poor defenders, Hammer included. They attacked the defence, wide and central, teasing the zone marking, trying to prise it open.

Across the way, Gavin was running riot, sending shot after shot in on the overworked goalkeeper. The session lasted three-quarters of an hour; shooting, then in turn taking on a player and defending in return.

'Hold the ball. Attract the defender. Get him in close. Play the ball in behind him. Timing! Timing! It's all about timing!'

Over with the others, Hammer and Cyril Stevens were under pressure from the first-team hotshots, Their pace was unbelievable. Their control instantaneous. What was more they reacted that split second quicker than Hammer and Cyril were used to. Theirs was a high power game, lightning quick, with instant reaction. It wasn't easy to keep up with the sleight of speed of the first-team forwards.

'It'll come, kids. Someday you'll be up there with the big shots.'

After the session John Warner and Sam Gregson went for a cup of coffee together. They were the best of friends. Whatever would happen in the future there would be no grudges, no recriminations.

As for Gavin and Hammer and the rest of the players, there would be the luxury of a shower. Leave the training-gear on the dressing-room table to be laundered, get ready to go out into 'civvy street', and have the rest of the day off.

Riverside were suspended from the Dublin Schoolboys League pending an inquiry. But much to Lar Holmes's disappointment they were quickly reinstated. A local priest from the St Peter's Parish of Little Bray had got in touch with the League.

'They're lovely lads.'

'Not from what we're hearing.'

'Live and let live. We're all God's creatures. They adore football. It would break their little hearts if you didn't allow them play in your league.'

Father Bourke was the priest's name. He carried out trojan work among the youth of the area, and was well liked. He had a soft, mesmerizing almost hypnotic West of Ireland accent. He could be very persuasive, especially over the phone, as he was now with the Dublin Schoolboys official.

'We'll see, Father. I'll bring the matter up at executive level. Though the lack of dressing-rooms would be a major problem.'

'I'm certain a parishioner could come up with the use of a garage or an outhouse.'

'That would be a big help, Father. Only other problem would be the horses.'

'Horses?'

'There's some kid down there with a drove of horses.'

'Sure that'll be simple to overcome. Haven't horses got legs? All that has to be done is move them.'

'Right, Father. We'll look into the matter straightway.'

'God bless you, sir.'

'And you too, Father. Keep in touch.'

Father Bourke gently replaced the phone on the receiver. He could only see one outcome: Riverside Boys U-14s would be back in action in the Dublin and District Schoolboys League. Through his youth work Father Bourke had come into contact with a lot of Riverside players over the years. Sure some of the players were from the immediate vicinity. Born on St Peter's Road,

31

attended St Peter's National School, worshipped at St Peter's Church, and would be buried in St Peter's cemetery.

If their christian names were Peter the circle would be perfected.

The thought brought tears to Father Bourke's eyes. He heaved a sigh and offered up a prayer: 'God bless their little souls.'

4

Word came back sooner than expected from London on Scorpion Jack's demo-tape. Jake produced the letter during a band practice at the Green Door, a rock-club at the Albert Walk in Bray.

'Give's a look.'

They all wanted to see it. Take it in their hands, examine it. They could hardly believe it was for real.

'It doesn't say much.'

'It doesn't have to. It's an introductory letter. Just to say the record company is interested and they're sendin' a representative over to hear us play.'

Big Red, the Green Door's bouncer wasn't long in getting in on the act. 'Don't forget me. I've done me bit to keep you on the road. Remember, I got you in here for band practice.'

'Yeah,' sneered Jake, 'we won't forget you. A two week all expenses paid holiday to John O'Gods.'

'That's not funny.'

'When's the rep comin' over?'

'Three weeks time. We're giggin' at the Baggot Inn. We're to ring the record company to set the whole thing up.'

'We're movin' at last!'

'Straight into the big-time!'

'Gear!'

'Class!'

'Magno!'

Jake slid the letter into his hip pocket, but Kev snatched it out.

'Give it back.'

'I want to show it to my Da.'

They all wanted to show the letter around town.

'Big deal. So what?'

Jake gave in.

Never before had they felt so excited. They got in behind their gear for a practice-jam. They were totally elated. The music belted out – each quaver, each chord, had a life of its own. *Daniel*, an Elton John number, ran strong and true in the dull after-hours light of the Green Door. Then the words of another Elton John song: *He ain't heavy ... He's my brother.* Powerful and emotional. Scorpion Jack could certainly transmit.

One of Jake and Dave's numbers followed: *Thunderbolt*, a fast rock compilation:

Thunderbolt... on fire... loco... the one that got away...

Three weeks' time and Scorpion Jack would be the ones getting away, career wise.

Like a bolt out of the blue... Thunderbolt!

Big Red sat at the back of the Green Door nodding his approval. Scorpion Jack were a good band. They had to be to make Big Red bop his head.

When Elaine was signing for Juventus, the club had baited her with talk of a modelling career to supplement her football income. But the promises were not quite what they seemed and Elaine soon realized that a modelling career would have meant an unbelieveable workload. Up at six o'clock most mornings, preparations, fittings, travelling, shows, photographic sessions – it would just not be possible to make it dovetail with her footballing routine. And with no prior training or experience of the modelling scene, her success would have been problematic in any event. No, Juventus had pulled a fast one in that respect. Talk of strutting the catwalks with models like Claudia Schiffer and Naomi Campbell was something of a joke really. She would never get to model Le Copains designer outfits, never visit the great Milan houses, except maybe to watch one of the spring fashion shows on TV. And maybe it would be the better option, to snuggle up in front of the fire and watch TV as the snow-laden winds blew in off the Alps from the Col de Mont Cenis and Mont Blanc, a reminder to the citizens of Turin and Milan that the worst hardships in life were French.

The representative from the London record company took in Scorpion's Jack's gig at the Baggot Inn. When it was over they all went to the Pink Elephant for an analysis of the demo-tape. Minerals were ordered and Scorpion Jack sat back to hear the verdict.

'I don't know exactly how to put this…' stalled the rep in an uncertain Oxford Blue accent.

'What d'ya mean?' Jake was beginning to feel edgy. All wasn't sunshine and roses, so to speak.

'Well, there are a few problems. Before going any further, I want to make one thing clear. This is a company viewpoint based mainly on the demo-tape.'

Jake looked to Liam. Liam to Kev, Kev to Dave. There was going to be bad news. Why go to the bother of sending a rep over from London then?

'There's a problem with the rhythm section… in the sense that we don't like the drummer.'

The words were like a hammer-blow to Liam. Totally unexpected. They didn't like the drummer. Bloody Hell!

'On playing back the demo-tape our experts feel your drummer doesn't keep a steady beat. I'm afraid he's just not good enough.'

Talk about being insensitive! The record company rep certainly was not the person from whom to hear about a death in the family.

'There's another problem. We'd also want to replace the

rhythm guitarist.'

That would be Kev gone. Life had just dealt him another cruel blow. And it showed.

Jake could see Scorpion Jack disintegrating before his very eyes.

'The company have a replacement rhythm guitarist in mind. He projects a great image. We'd be lucky to have him on board.'

'A bloody hatchet job,' quaked Liam. He felt like hitting the Limey, or Spiv, or whatever he was.

The company rep took a short sip from his Pernod, stroked the glass and spoke directly to Jake and Dave. 'We like your music. Got much more material?'

'Plenty.'

'Same style?'

'Mostly.'

'The Company would like both of you to come over to London in a few weeks' time. They want to try out a new drummer, also the rhythm guitarist I mentioned. They want to see how you hit it off together. They'd shop you out to a few gigs. Maybe the Town and Country. Maybe the Marquee. If the gigs go well you'd be contracted to record an album.'

'Can you not take a chance? Don't split the group… do it as we are?'

'No way. The Company want to bring in replacements.'

'We'll think it over.'

'Take a week. Want my number?'

'Yeah, sure.'

The record company rep gave Jake his phone number. Liam was fuming. Kev looked devastated. Two kids' dreams of fame were shattered. It was all right for the record company rep – he wouldn't be around to pick up the pieces. He would be on the early morning flight back to London. What really hurt, though, was the fact that the record company didn't believe they were good enough.

36

It was especially bad for Kev. His father had done everything he could to keep Scorpion Jack going. He had gone out of his way to help. Jake and Dave knew it wouldn't be easy to face him if they decided to take up the record company's offer and go to London.

On the way out of the Pink Elephant, Liam, who had a ferocious temper, gave vent to his disappointment. He kicked a chair, and if there had been a pink elephant around he would have half crippled it. It was his second disappointment in a month. Up until lately he had helped to produce a children's radio show. Out of the blue it got axed; they were just going on air when they were told the bad news. Uncle Bob's show had been going for years and was loved by all the kids who tuned in. Those who worked on it were never paid a red cent for all the years they had put in. They did it on a voluntary basis, taking satisfaction in the enormous pleasure it gave its listeners.

'Boys and girls, this is Uncle Bob. Though it may be wet and cold outside I hope you enjoy the show. Sadly, boys and girls, all things must come to an end. But think of the great times we've had, and all the songs and jokes, and the seagull that circles the sky and brings back news of who's good and bad, who's sick and sad. Boys and girls, this is our last show.'

Twenty minutes later a nine-year-old girl rang in. She recited a poem and signed off: 'Uncle Bob, we all love you.'

Although none of the listeners could see it, she had brought tears to Uncle Bob's eyes. Still on air, he thanked her and said, 'Liam, give us a drink of water there.' Only the water wasn't water; it was whiskey.

The show got more and more sentimental after that.

'And we have Liam here. He produces the show and plays the requests. A big thank-you to Liam. Been around since he was knee-high in short trousers. And Amanda. Boys and girls, when Amanda tells a story you think she reads it from a book. But she doesn't. She sits there and tells if from her head. Boys and girls, give Amanda a clap.'

Uncle Bob and The Last Radio Show. Christ! It stuck in the 'craw'.

The four lads shared a taxi home. Liam gave them some stick on the journey.

'We started out together. So we should stick together. I'm playin' drums since I was eleven. What does that English prat know about drummers? What do you say? We stick together?'

Kev had nothing to add. He just stared zombie-like out of the taxi window.

Neither Jake nor Dave bothered to reply. There was too much at stake. Scorpion Jack was finished. Liam knew it. Kev knew it. There was no point in arguing about a foregone conclusion. Just sit back in the taxi and eat their hearts out, thinking of what might have been. Funny thing, the dark. If you're lucky you can't see anything.

Nothing much was happening for Luke on the jobs front. Apart from the FÁS course, everything was a dead-end. Though Gavin's father had got him a temporary job working with him on the buildings, Luke knew it wouldn't last. The job was menial, making tea and tidying up on the site.

While it lasted, Gavin's father could see Luke was handy at carpentry.

'You should get yourself apprenticed. Either that, or go to England and say you've work experience. You'd get a job on the buildings over there, no bother. That's what I did when I was a kid – worked on the buildings in England. Made a man of me – helped get me priorities right. None of this going to discos or foolin' around with me. I worked hard as a kid. Sixteen years I did in England. When I went over I had next to no work experience. I was willin' to try anythin'. Do this? Do that?

How were they to know? I had a go at everythin' on offer.

'Luke, you're not bad at carpentry. Why don't you chuck those pigeons in and take the boat. Gavin'd let you stay with him. Good lad, Gavin. Hasn't forgotten his roots nor his family. Gavin'd look after you. I'll get his mother to drop him a line sayin' you're goin' over.'

'I don't think so, Mr Byrne.'

'Never mind the "Mr". Call me Jimmy. It's time you broke out an' did somethin' for yourself. If you don't do it soon you'll be stuck in a rut for life.'

'I don't want to go to work in England, Mr. Byrne.'

'Suit yourself. But it doesn't look as if there's much for you here.'

Prophetic words. Come winter and the job was gone. There were too many wet days, too many working hours lost through rain. He began to sign on at the 'Labour'. Apart from his pigeons, all he had in life was his dole money and a fistful of EU butter vouchers. Always introspective, he began to retreat even more into himself. Bar his pigeons, he didn't care any more.

Father Bourke hadn't been sleeping on the Riverside issue. He came up trumps and got the boys reinstated in the Dublin Schoolboys League.

'Bless you,' he thanked the Dublin Schoolboys official. The official was hardly 'blessed' – more likely cursed with Riverside back in the League.

Fair play to Father Bourke, he had done all the donkey work in advance. He had arranged for Riverside, and their anticipated opposition, to tog out in the garage of a house just across the road from the Park. The house owner was an ex-footballer himself. He had played in goal for Drumcondra AFC. Drumcondra in those days had played in the League of Ireland, out of Tolka Park.

There was just the one problem with Riverside's new dressing-rooms. There was no toilet. Riverside always got worked up before a match – especially an important league or cup game. They were always on the run to relieve themselves.

'Mister, can we use your toilet.'

'I don't want any of you lot using my toilet.'

'Why not?'

'You'll rob the house blind.'

'Mister, we're not delinquents, we're footballers. Ever hear of footballers robbin' houses?'

'Okay, you can use the toilet. But only in an emergency.'

'If it's not an emergency, what do we do?'

'Go behind one of the trees in the Park. And you're not to wear your boots in the house.'

'Okay, Mister. Anythin' you say, Mister. Can we have a wash after the match?'

'Definitely not!'

The house rules were set. It was up to Riverside to observe them.

Rules? Riverside didn't know the meaning of the word.

Not only had Father Bourke found a dressing-room for Riverside, he had also sorted out Chopper Doyle.

He rang Wicklow County Council. The official was helpful.

'We'll send a truck straight down and have the horses impounded.'

As luck would have it, Lar Holmes, Sean Dunlop and Eddie Reilly were called to the Park to help round up the horses and load them on to a horse transporter. In fact not one but two.

Luckily Chopper Doyle wasn't to be seen. He was on an afternoon trip to nearby Leopardstown Racecourse, to have a look over the fences in the hope that he'd be allowed to enter a race someday soon.

'Chopper, you just can't go to Leopardstown and race. You have to become a jockey, and have a jockey's licence.'

'I'll become a jockey then.'

'You'll have to get in with a stables. Approach a trainer

and ride from experience.'

'I get plenty of experience ridin' in the Park.'

'It's not that kind of experience you need.'

'Bull! If I wanna race, I'll race. Doncaster, Cheltenham, Aintree. If I wanna race I'll be there. Nobody'll stop me.'

It wasn't easy to stop Chopper. He was a person of conviction.

But Lar Holmes, Sean Dunlop, Eddie Reilly, and the rest of the Wicklow County Council crew stopped him, at least temporarily. They rounded up his troupe of stray horses and brought them off to the Council pound near Wicklow Town.

Chopper was devastated. But Father Bourke, afraid he might go off the rails and get into trouble, got in touch with him. Took him to one side and instructed him with some words of wisdom.

He also used his influence with a reputable racing stables on the Curragh. Next thing, Chopper was off to Kildare to serve as an apprentice jockey. The People's Park was finally rid of stray horses.

Like the salmon that threaded the Dargle, Chopper was gone to the sea of his dreams. And like the salmon he would only make one yearly visit to the town of his birth.

Before he left he scrawled a message on the gable-end of the town's Heritage Centre:

CHOPPER DOYLE RULES
CHOPPER DOYLE OK

All that was missing was the sound of hoof-beats as Chopper rode off into the sunset.

But he would get plenty of that on the Curragh.

5

Sam Gregson was bringing the reserves along nicely, without exactly setting the League on fire. It wasn't easy managing a reserve team. Matters seldom ran to plan, a problem not just confined to London Albion. It was the same with most other clubs.

Sam Gregson had made a few changes to the team, one of which was to play Gavin up front all the time. His days of playing midfield were past tense. His future with London Albion lay totally in a striker's role. Physically, Gavin, Hammer, Mick Bates and Cyril Stevens, all players who had graduated through the Youth-team system, had come on a ton. Much of the credit had to be given to Bill Thornbull, their trainer from their Youth-team days. Bill had toned their muscles over the last few years with gym-work. Sadly, in the modern game, players had to be physically endowed.

John Warner, the first-team manager, constantly checked the reserves' progress, Gavin and Mick Bates in particular. He was also showing great interest in Cyril Stevens and Hammer, who were developing a great central defensive partnership. They showed perfect understanding, and complemented one another's game inside out; there was no way a defensive mix-up could result between them. They were a masterful pair: Hammer with his sleeves rolled up, and an intensity of purpose in every tackle, every move, every stylish clearance; Cyril Stevens, immaculate, a thoroughbred, who made everything he did look effortless, graceful. When it came to centre-halves, he was a Rolls-Royce type of player. But there wasn't much chance of either of them making the first team, not yet. Not while Paul Smith and

Scotch Pete were around. Both were among the top centre-halves in the Premiership. Scotch Pete, in particular, was a cult figure in London Albion – a legend with the fans. No, Hammer and Cyril Stevens would have to wait a while to displace that pair.

'We'll be old men before we get their places.'

'Scotch Pete's gettin' on,' argued Cyril Stevens. 'It might be sooner than you think.'

'What about Paul Smith?'

'What about him? He can't go on forever.'

'We can't wait forever,' added Hammer glumly.

'Know what's wrong with you?' retorted Cyril.

'What?'

'You're lackin' in confidence.'

'Funny, Gavin's always sayin' the same.'

'Time you pulled yourself together, the way you do on the pitch. Believe in yourself. Dress trendy. Show yourself off.'

'You must be jokin'.'

'Look at Dwight Crawford. He's always showin' himself off.'

'Not doin' him much good.'

'Think not? Plays on the first team. Gets on TV, in the papers. He gets himself noticed. You should do the same?

'What's this, football or showbusiness?'

'Both.'

'I'll stick to the football.'

Hammer was Hammer. He'd never change.

The two people Lar Holmes detested most in life were from Bray. One was Mr Glynn, the manager of Riverside Boys U-14s; the other was the infamous Harry Hennessy, referee and Riverside's secret weapon when the going got tough on the playing fields down Dargle-side.

Harry Hennessy was an official referee. In Lar Holmes's eyes, too fat, too fond of drink and an absolute cheat when refereeing; there was only one team he favoured and that was Riverside Boys.

A few months earlier, his refereeing career had been dealt a mortal blow. In July, all the Wicklow branch referees had to undergo a fitness test and an oral examination regarding the rules of the game. The tests were held at Greystones Rugby Club.

Harry knew straightway he was in trouble. The Referees' Inspector, a horrible man, was present. This man was going to kick him out of football – strip him of being a referee. Take away his referee's badge. Throw his notebook and whistle in the dustbin, so to speak. But Harry would show him. He'd trot and sprint with the best. He'd have all the correct answers when it came to the oral test.

But poor Harry didn't get as far as the oral test. It was sheer hell doing the physical. In the sprints, the sweat poured off him, and as hard as he tried his legs couldn't gather up enough momentum to get him beyond a slow crawl. He got so red that nobody would have been surprised if he had exploded. As for lapping, that wasn't so much an ordeal as an impossibility. He failed hands down.

'Get that man out of here,' shouted the Referees' Inspector.

Harry was helped, exhausted and humiliated, back to the dressing-rooms.

The Inspector gave him the bad news straight off.

'No more refereeing, you're gone. About four stone overweight. Get yourself sorted out, man, before it's too late.'

Talk of insensitivity! Harry was in tears, only the sweat camouflaged the tiny droplets.

'Bastard!'

He took off his official referee's outfit and sadly placed it in his black leather hold-all. He had a shower. Dressed and went upstairs to the club bar. He ordered a Guinness, sat down and looked out of the wide window of the pavilion at what was going on outside.

He wasn't really interested. He felt numb. Afterwards, the others came up and offered their commiserations. One of them gave him a lift back to Bray and dumped him on the Lower Dargle Road outside his favourite pub. He felt like crossing the road into the Park and throwing his football bag into the river. He had second thoughts. Throw his referee's outfit away? Never! He lovingly clutched the bag under his arm, walked into the pub, and got sloshed.

Lar Holmes was, understandably, over the moon at the decision.

Lar's other pet aversion was Mr Glynn. They had been soccer adversaries for years, and had even played at junior level against one another. There wasn't much of a dislike in those days – they were just lads, enjoying life. But once they both got involved in football management attitudes changed and a kind of hatred, due to being in opposition, developed. It wasn't very deep-rooted, just on the surface.

Perhaps rivalry was a more correct term to use. In the old days Mr Glynn had an old banger of a car (an Opel). But now he had a brand new Toyota Corolla saloon. When he had the Opel he used to cram the players in and drive to matches. He had even used it as a dressing-room. But that kind of carry-on was totally out of order with the Toyota. Nowadays when Riverside played away from home they always travelled in a hired minibus. For home matches and training sessions they used 'Shanks's mare'. The days of abusing Mr Glynn's private transport were over as far as Riverside's U-14s were concerned.

Harry Hennessy's removal from the refereeing scene was a definite 'downer' for Mr Glynn and Riverside Boys. Harry wouldn't be around any more to give them crucial match-winning decisions. But the Harry Hennessy saga wasn't over yet; Mr Glynn got him to help out with the U-14s. The sight of the two men together galled Lar Holmes. It was just as well Shamrock Boys and Riverside weren't competing in the same section of the League. There would have been bedlam on the sideline with, perhaps, some of the players mischievously adding to the confrontation. If ever there was a match made both in Heaven and Hell it was the combination of Mr Glynn, Harry Hennessy and Riverside's U-14s.

As Father Bourke would fervently say, 'God bless their little souls.'

The People's Park always filled Harry Hennessy with nostalgia. He was usually full of nostalgia and Guinness. Soccer-wise, the Park certainly was a special place. Legends like Tommy Hamilton, Andy McEvoy, Alan Kelly, and 'lesser lights' whose names never quite made the big-time, all learned the basics in the Park.

He and Mr Glynn had fond memories of them all.

'Remember Robbie Stevens?'

'Will I ever forget?'

Just as Gavin and Hammer were special in the annals of Shamrock Boys, so too was this particular player in the folklore of Riverside Boys. Like Gavin, he went on to play schoolboy football for Ireland, and also to play in the English League.

'Remember him coming into the Park with his football gear in one hand and holding his little sister with the other?'

'He never spoke about football. But he was never out of the Park. He lived here, whether playin' or watchin'. There was always one place you'd find Robbie Stevens, and that was in the Park.'

'Robbie was a great player.'

'The best we ever had.'

Another pause for thought.

'Remember the old iron goalposts?'

'The ones Teddy Fitzgerald made?'

Teddy Fitzgerald was a blacksmith and wrought-iron specialist by trade. And highly skilled. He was the administrator for schoolboy soccer in the area. Robby Stevens had had a nickname for him: 'Teddy Horseshoes.'

'Remember when Teddy told us all with pride that the Council was going to resod the whole bottom half of the Park, and when things would be ready there'd be a junior and schoolboy pitch on it?'

'That's what Teddy said. Sure didn't the GAA go to the Town Hall and get the junior pitch for themselves. The schoolboy pitch was shoved into a corner at the bottom of the Park. Leftovers, that's what we got.'

'Poor old Teddy Fitzgerald stood up to the Town Hall though.'

'They took the pitch off him all the same.'

'But we got it all back in end.'

'Sure, only because the GAA got sick of the place and got somewhere better.'

'Remember the dog Teddy used to have?'

'Mutt.'

'The kids all said that Teddy and Mutt used to pick the schoolboy League selection between them.'

'That's right. Robbie Stevens always said Teddy would mention a name and if Mutt wagged his tail the player'd be on the team.'

'It was awful what happened to Mutt.'

'Yeah, some bloody mad driver flattened him all over the top of the Killarney Road.'

Whatever about dogs, football, my friend, is all about memories.

6

Elaine was really hitting top form. Fourteen goals in ten games. Her technical skills had come on a lot in the last six months. What was more, Juventus toughened her physique beyond recognition. It was almost impossible to knock her off the ball. In addition, she had really settled in to the Italian way of life. So much so, that when her Dad wrote to her saying an athletic scholarship had come through from Providence in Rhode Island she didn't in the least care that she would miss it; as far as she was concerned she had made the correct choice in going to Italy. Turin was football mad. There was nothing as fulfilling as playing in front of the Juventus masses with their fervour of passion and gaily-coloured club banners, some of which read:

Juventus Club G. Scirea Busca.

Juventus Club Salerno.

Juventus Club Borgo Vittoria.

No wonder Juventus was the best supported club in Italy. It had supporters all over the country. And if it was known you played for Juventus ... well, you just couldn't go wrong.

And there would be the added pleasure of going skiing in the Alps. Skiing – Elaine could hardly wait.

One of the biggest kicks she got was when she was asked to do some promotional work for Juventus. She was sent to a shopping precinct, and who was there only Roberto Baggio. They stood side by side while the Italian press took photographs. Roberto Baggio! That was really cool. She sent some of the photos back home.

Italy was a dream and Elaine couldn't have been happier.

Luke Doyle was a quiet, introverted type of person. Those who didn't know him thought he was slightly weird. Lately, he had let his hair grow long and had taken to wearing a khaki coloured combat-jacket, with the legend 'Peace' and a dove emblazoned on it.

Luke's parents were on the verge of despair, although they didn't let it show in front of him. Bar Jake, Gavin and Hammer from the 'old days' he didn't seem to have any friends, nor want any. He was a total loner. Something was eating away inside him. There was a log-jam of pent-up emotion. It wasn't easy to talk to him nor for him to take another person into his confidence. If he had problems he wouldn't tell anyone, not even Jake. He kept everything bottled up inside.

It was hard to figure out why he was like that. Maybe he was born that way – born with a flaw that was progressively getting worse. Maybe it was the fact that he hadn't had a real job since he left school Maybe it eroded his confidence, his dignity.

Most mornings he spent with his pigeons, then maybe watch TV or go out along the Cliff Walk that straddled the coastline between Bray and Greystones. He had always spent a lot of time along its beaten track looking for stray pigeons. But that was usually during the pigeon-racing season, between May and September. Now he was up there in the middle of winter, in rain, wind or snow.

Lately, his concentration was going to pot. The previous week he had gone into a pet-shop in Bray to purchase a bottle of Duramitex.

'Durex,' he asked the shop owner.

'Get out!'

Two women customers in the shop were totally disgusted. 'Durex! Did you ever hear the likes?'

Luke didn't realize the slippage of words, not until he got outside. He wanted to go back into the shop to apologise but the shop-owner was glaring at him through the window. He decided to give the Duramitex a miss.

He'd get someone to get it for him some other time.

Not only was he having lapses in concentration, he had a recurring nightmare of a man wringing pigeons' necks and throwing them into a barrel. Luke knew the source of the nightmare; it had happened a few years earlier when he and Jake had gone into Bray to fetch a few pigeons from an old man who was getting out of the fancy. The nightmare was recurring a lot lately. Sometimes in the middle of the night, he'd wake up, covered in sweat. Worse: sometimes when he was out along the Cliff Walk he'd sit passively among the folds of his cumbersome jacket and stare at the white flecks of spray beating off the cliffs. He'd sit and stare for what only seemed like seconds, but in reality was about twenty minutes or half-an-hour. And in the white spray of the waves, the nightmare would haunt him again.

He kept his nightmares to himself. He told no one. He kept them in his head and wouldn't let them out. He was slowly cracking up.

Jake was worried about Luke. Particularly when Luke told him that he spent a lot of time down along the railway track that ran below the Cliff Walk. And in the tunnels. That really raised the hair on Jake's neck. In the tunnels he could so easily be struck by a speeding train. He had tried to help. Without putting any pressure on Luke or making him suspicious, he often asked him to travel to gigs gratis free with Scorpion Jack, but the invitation was usually declined. The few times he did go Jake tried to get him fixed up with some of the girls that followed the band, in an effort to try to get him to unwind. But the girl scenario didn't work with Luke. He'd always freeze, completely clam up, and the girls would lose interest.

Perhaps in the ordinary way Jake would have been more conscious of Luke's deteriorating mental condition. But the impending break with Scorpion Jack and the London invitation were occupying all his thoughts.

Jake and Dave accepted the offer from London. Scorpion Jack were dead. Their loyal fans were demoralized, although at the same time delighted that Jake and Dave had attracted one of the top record companies on the British and international market. After the initial disappointment Kev and Liam didn't take matters too badly either. In retrospect, they couldn't blame the two lads. It was an opportunity that had to be grasped. Jake and Dave's song-writing abilities deserved to have an international platform. In the end there were no hard feelings, just a sense of good-will and a hope that the lads would do well in London. Anyway, all would not be doom and gloom. Kev and Liam were to front a new band, one that was quite capable of making a comfortable crust on the Irish scene.

Scorpion Jack decided to play one last gig together as a thank-you to their local supporters who had followed the band through thick and thin since the early days. Although small, the most appropriate place to have the gig was the Green Door. It was to be hush-hush; more of a private affair. But word wasn't long in getting out. News spread quickly on the grapevine, and a full two hours before the gig was due to begin the whole Albert Walk area, which fronted the Green Door, was chock-a-block with Scorpion Jack fans.

The police had to be called in

Crush barriers were erected.

Big Red was to the fore, standing directly in front of the Green Door, arms folded, defying the crowd.

'I ain't seen crowds like this since I was a whipper-snapper. Reminds me of the time I went to the Roxy to see Elvis in *Jailhouse Rock*. The show turned into a riot. Squad-cars turned up from all over. One half of the crowd jived in the aisles; the other half slugged it out with the cops. Some night! The best night of me life.'

'I bet you were the first to be arrested,' jibed a heavily

sloganned Scorpion Jack fan.

'No, the management was very impressed. They offered me the bouncer's job the next day.'

'Why? Did the old bouncer chuck in?'

'No, someone threw him over the balcony, an' he hadn't a parachute. Some crowd here. Did you know, Bob Geldof and the Boomtown Rats used to gig in Bray before they became famous?'

'No.'

'Nobody much ever went to their gigs. They never once needed a bouncer in Bray.'

'You're jokin'.'

'No. The only bouncer they ever got was a dud cheque.'

By this time the local Garda Superintendent had come on the scene. The crowd, although orderly, was much too large for public safety. The whole set-up was out of order. The Superintendent had a quick word with his fellow officers. A phone-call was made to the Chairman of Bray Urban District Council. A few more phone-calls followed, one to a local electrical engineer.

The Green Door was declared out of bounds. In the interest of public safety the gig was moved to the bandstand on Bray seafront. There was precious little time to set up the band equipment, about three-quarters of an hour.

The crowd moved from the Albert Walk, down to the seafront, followed by a newly arrived local entrepreneur in a crocked-up fish-'n'-chip van.

The entrepreneur was the focus for a slagging from a section of the crowd.

'Where's your tax-disc?'

'In the post.'

'Your insurance?'

'In the post.'

'You use the post a lot.'

'Sure, helps keep the overheads down. I'm in business to make money, not dole it out.'

'Hope you got the cat-food on standby.'

'What for?'

'For the battered burgers. Me mates got a few off you last week. They haven't stopped meowin' since.'

'Don't forget, when you get enough money together, buy an engine for the van. Your girl friend'll die of a heart-attack shovin' it around the place.'

'There's nothin' wrong with my van.'

'No, nothin'. Except it would be better off with legs.'

The banter went on. The electrical engineer was working double quick to spotlight the bandstand and get the acoustics into shape. The crowd began to chant for Scorpion Jack to come onstage. Big Red circled the edge of the bandstand egging on the crowd to greater peals of support. Scorpion Jack wouldn't be long. They were putting the finishing touches to their stage wardrobe, getting ready back at the Green Door. They were due to walk the length of the Albert Walk on to the seafront under the protection of a gardai escort. Talk about triumphalism! All that would be missing was the ghetto-blaster quaking of 'Eye of the Tiger'. That would really smash them, especially Big Red. He was an ex-boxer. Champion of the bar room. He had fought many a title fight in his day, none of them in the roped ring.

While the crowd waited for Scorpion Jack, Big Red lorded it centre stage. He was something of a folk-hero among the local kids. He picked up a mike, told a few stories about the good old days. He even sang a song. It was brutal. Sentimental mush, that probably only the dead could comprehend; like most hard-hitting whiskey drinkers, he was a sentimentalist. He loved the seafront. As a youth he had patrolled the place night and day in his best drain-pipe trousers, velvet jacket, periwinkle shoes, long locks, sleek, wavy Brylcreemed DA hairstyle. The seafront was a monument to his youth, especially the duke-boxes at the Fun Palace and at the Bray Head end where the Casino once stood.

Duane Eddy, Fats Domino, Elvis Presley; they were the closest that Big Red ever came to culture.

At present, on the bandstand, another piece of culture was slowly approaching Big Red; namely Sergeant McGrath, whose retirement papers must have got lost in the Customs House fire during the Civil War. Big Red and Sergeant McGrath went back a long way, to the days when Big Red occasionally attended primary school. Sergeant McGrath was a big man and in the old days he used a bike to get around. On account of being a bigger than average person he had something akin to a motorbike saddle to sit himself down on while he cycled. One day, during school hours, Big Red was sitting on a wall somewhere along the Sidmonton Road as Sergeant McGrath cycled by. Big Red got an urge to pass a remark. The urge was so strong, he just couldn't resist it, regardless of the consequences.

'Hey, Sarge! Watch out the saddle doesn't slip up your behind!'

Sergeant McGrath wheeled around with surprising speed and pedalled back. He dragged Big Red in behind the wall and gave him a good thumping. That was the day Big Red found out he could take a punch; a very crucial development in any boxer's life. Big Red didn't pass any more comments in the Sergeant's direction after that. Well, not unless he had a good uphill distance between himself and the Sergeant. The Sergeant was no King of the Mountains. He may have been good on the sprints, but he was a dead loss on the hills.

On this occasion Sergeant McGrath wasn't long in approaching Big Red on the bandstand and telling him to belt up and not be upsetting the crowd. Reluctantly Big Red handed over the microphone to a local DJ who took over the *persona* of Master of Ceremonies.

Introductions were dispensed with. Scorpion Jack came onstage. Straightway they got the crowd going. Jake stalked across the stage, half jerking, half twisting his body in strong, deliberate movements. He held his guitar in the hip position, pointing to the crowd, the strong rock music machine-gunning the front of the bandstand with its loudness. Dave wasn't far behind. He moved to the right of Jake at a slightly shallower angle. Kev kept an anchor position just to the edge of a spotlight that beamed on to Liam flaying the drums.

'Give's Meat Loaf.'

Scorpion Jack obliged.

Dave took lead vocals.

Jake and Kev came on strong with a powerful guitar back-up. Liam paced the beat of the drums beautifully.

'Who's yer man said Liam couldn't keep the beat?'

'Never mind. English twits! Only want to get their own lads in on the act.'

'Give's one of Scorpion Jack's numbers. One of yer best.'

'How about three of the best,' retorted Jake, nodding to Kev who led into the opening bars of a Scorpion Jack power-blaster.

Apart from a few twinkling houselights Bray Head was shielded in darkness. The first of the three selected Scorpion Jack numbers blasted the length of the seafront, from the pure darkness of the Head to the grey slabs of the harbour wall. Three of the best from Scorpion Jack! The crowd were immersed in the exclusiveness of the occasion. Bodies swayed, hands punched the air at every elevation of tone. With each change of note, each upbeat of tempo, the musical rhythm interacted. The crowd and Scorpion Jack became as one. Girls became hysterical. Fellows freaked out. Soon as the last number would be played Scorpion Jack would be no more. But their music would live on. Jake and Dave would see to that. Maybe there would be new faces – a different band but the music would always be Jake and Dave's. The soul would still be the same.

Then a hush came over the crowd and Scorpion Jack were about to play their last number as a group. It was a song of Jake's:

> *'... be a friend*
> *For as long as it takes,*
> *As long as it shapes.*
> *Be together*
> *Whenever you want,*
> *Whenever you need.*
> *Be a friend*
> *For as long as it takes,*
> *As long as it is...'*

As soon as the last chord faded, life for Scorpion Jack as a band was over. Scorpion Jack was dead. Long live Rock and Roll.

The London Albion club fanzine, *Terrace Space*, was one of the most highly regarded in the Premiership. It sold like hot-cakes at all the first team's home games. Ricky Lee, the fanzine's editor, had a soft spot for Gavin. Already he had profiled him as the star of the Youth team which had won the FA Youth Cup.

Mick Bates had just featured in an open question-and-answer article, so Ricky thought it was time to put Gavin under the spotlight again in a special two-page feature.

'Where did you play your first football?'

'The Railway Field, Greystones.'

'Why is it called the Railway Field?'

'The trains pass it.'

'Any in particular?'

'The Dublin-Rosslare Express.'

'Rosslare? That's Wexford.'

'Yeah. The Fishguard ferry goes from there.'

'Did you come over from Ireland on the ferry?'

'No, I flew over from Dublin.'

'The Railway Field – the trains. It sounds good. Can you give me an angle I can work into the article? A linkage that might interest the fans?'

'Well, the Dublin-Rosslare Express passes Lansdowne

Road, where all the big soccer internationals are played.'

'And some day you'd like to play for Ireland?'

'Of course.'

'And it also goes by the Railway Field?'

'Yes.'

'It'll fit in … Any brothers?'

'Just one.'

'What's his name?'

'Garry.'

'Any good at football?'

'Reasonable. He plays schoolboy. U-14. Plays for the same manager I started out with.'

'What's his name?'

'Lar Holmes.'

'Father play soccer?'

'I don't think he was very good.'

'Where did you get it from then?'

'My grandfather, on my mother's side. He was from Ringsend, in Dublin.'

'Tell me a bit about him.'

So Gavin told Ricky about his grandad and Ringsend Park. Gavin's grandad had played for Shamrock Rovers, with players like Ronnie Nolan, Paddy Coade, Paddy Ambrose. He played in the European Cup against Man Utd. Just before the Munich air disaster. Got beaten 0–6 at Dalymount Park; 3-2 at Old Trafford in the return leg. He had never played as a full international though. The zenith of his representative honours was a handful of Inter-League Caps against the English, Scottish and Irish Leagues.

'Your grandad, was he a full-time professional?'

'No, part-time.'

'What did he work at?'

'A docker, unloadin' coal from ships. The coal came in at Ringsend, that was where he worked.'

'Know anything about the coal-ships?'

'Not really, except that they were from Poland. As a kid

grandad used to root through the coal-tips for "sparklers", lumps of coal that could ignite, and bring them to the office and the girl'd give him two pence for every "sparkler". The coal had to be hosed down regularly to prevent fires.'

'Sounds interesting. I think we've enough ... Gavin, there's a big buzz going around the club lately. Haven't you noticed?'

'Not really.'

'The buzz is all about you. We'll be featuring you in the fanzine a little more often.'

'Think Dwight Crawford'll mind?'

'Hump him. He's a good player, but too much of an exhibitionist. Let him stew another while.'

Gavin thanked Ricky, and made off down the corridor for a cup of coffee and a chat with Mrs Dawson, the tea-lady. An article in the club fanzine! That meant the hard-core London Albion fans were all on his side. If popularity meant anything he'd be on the first team in a matter of weeks. The more he thought about it the better he felt.

Life was on the up-and-up.

The London Albion hard-core fans weren't the only ones who appreciated Gavin Byrne. Aston Villa got in touch with John Warner.

'John, we know the kid's doing well on the reserves. Have you any plans to bring him into the first team? What I mean is, have you any use for him?'

'Of course I have. He's the best thing at this club. I just don't want to rush him, that's all.'

'I don't know if you remember, but we were mad keen on the kid as a schoolboy.'

'So I've been told.'

'We had him watched. Unfortunately, we weren't his choice. John, I'm badly stuck for a goalscorer. We'll give you £600,000 for his signature.'

'He's worth a lot more.'

'Not as an unproven player.'

'He's only unproven because I haven't decided to bring him on yet.'

'Still unproven. Until he goes out on the park and does the business for the first team nobody knows what he's capable of.'

'Probably capable of two million at least when that day comes.'

'I'll up the offer to £900,000.'

'Not on.'

'Maybe I should be talking to Ted Brinsley.'

'Do that. I wouldn't sell at any price. But then Ted wouldn't either. Look, my contract is up at the end of the season. He wants me to hold on with London Albion for another few years. Looking at it that way, he wouldn't want to upset me. You'd only be wasting your time talking to Ted Brinsley. The kid's not for sale.'

'Everybody has their price.'

'And so have I. If Ted Brinsley wants me to stay, the kid's part of the deal. If the kid goes, I'm gone.'

'So I'd be wasting my time talking to Ted Brinsley?'

'You sure would. A season of first-team football and Gavin Byrne would be worth three-and-a-half million pounds.'

'John?'

'What?'

'Forget it!'

'You too, until Gavin Byrne has played a full season in the Premiership.'

About two weeks before the end of November Luke cycled out the Cliff Walk towards Bray. It was quite easy to cycle the Cliff Walk, although the ground surface was rough and the path was narrow. He was on the watch-out for a certain pigeon – a grizzle. Luke had first noticed it the previous July. Its strength was sapped from one of the young-bird races and it never recovered the urge to make it back to its home loft. There had been another bird with it, but it had gone; either that or it had perished. But the grizzle had stayed on right through the summer, into the autumn.

Luke had been up on the Cliff Walk almost every Saturday and Sunday through the autumn, and had seen the grizzle often on the cliffs. He had even tracked it into Bray, down to the harbour, but he was never able to catch it. He had even discovered where it roosted, down off the slope of the Cliff Walk in a disused railway tunnel from which the railway line had been removed because of erosion by the sea. He had thought of going to the tunnel at night with a strong flashlight and a net, in the hope the startled pigeon would fly into the beam of light which could be placed directly behind the net (at night a startled bird will fly directly into a pool of light), but the slope to the tunnel was too dangerous to negotiate once darkness fell. He could have walked the railway line from Greystones, but that would be dangerous, far too dangerous, what with scheduled passenger trains on the single line, not to mention the shunting of engines between Bray and Greystones.

When Luke got to a certain point he chained his bike to the fence and climbed down on to the railway track. He walked in behind a ledge and there, just in off the dizzy fall into the sea, was the disused tunnel through which the old railway track used to run. He went into the tunnel. There was light, a gloomy dull light. He picked up a stone and threw it into the black void, up near the roof of the tunnel, where the pigeon usually roosted. There was no beat of wings, no startled flight from the tunnel out into daylight. The pigeon wasn't there.

Luke left the tunnel and got on his bike. He cycled on towards Bray, keeping an eye out on the cliffs and the slopes on both sides of the Cliff Walk. When he came to where the Walk ended he cycled down the concrete slope on to Bray Promenade, and along it to the harbour. He went down beside the boat-slip in the harbour to where the grit-bank was, but the pigeon wasn't there either. He went back up on to the harbour bridge and looked around. No sign. He checked the North Pier and the Back Strand. Still not a trace. He remounted his bike and rode back towards Greystones.

Back out on the Cliff Walk, about a mile from Bray, he came across a man in distress. He had sprained his ankle on the lumpy uneven ground and could hardly walk.

'Want help?' asked Luke.

'Yes, if you wouldn't mind. I turned on my ankle... I think it's only sprained, but I don't think I'll be able to make it back to my car.'

'Where's your car?'

'In the car-park beside the golf course, at the side of Bray Head.'

'If you like...' Luke felt a bit embarrassed by what he was about to say. After all, the man was well-dressed, obviously well-to-do. 'If you like... that's if you can't walk properly, I can give you a cross-bar back to your car.' He felt stupid, but what else could he say? The man was obviously in pain and could hardly stand.

The man looked at Luke. He didn't answer immediately, but when he did he accepted the offer.

Within five minutes they were back at the car-park. Luke helped the man get into his car, a BMW. But when he put his foot on the clutch he couldn't operate it. It was too badly sprained.

'I wonder if you'd do something else for me?'

Luke nodded.

'Please ring this Bray number. Whoever answers, tell them Mr Creamer has a difficulty. He sprained his ankle and can't drive home. Ask them to send someone to drive me home. Will you do that?'

He gave him a phone number and Luke went off on his bike to the nearest phone box and rang the number. He wasn't back five minutes when a car pulled into the car-park with two people in it. One got in behind the wheel of Mr Creamer's car.

'Thanks for your help,' said Mr Creamer to Luke. 'What age are you?'

'Eighteen.'

'Still at school?'

'No, finished.'

'Do your Leaving Cert?'

'Yes.'

'Looking for a job?'

'Yes.'

'Have you anything in mind?'

'No, just hoping.'

'Well,' said Mr Creamer, handing Luke a business card, 'ring this number and there'll be a job for you. I own a couple of food-processing factories – among other things. I have one right here in Bray.'

Luke looked at the card. It had a Dun Laoghaire phone-code – probably Dalkey.

Luke thanked him, hoping he had meant what he said. The car door closed and the two cars left the car-park. Mr Creamer was gone, on his way home.

Luke remounted his bicycle and pedalled back to Greystones. He never found the grizzle pigeon, but because of it he had a job lined up. One door never closes before another opens – so goes the saying; so it goes – or something like that.

And, as he was to find out later, it wasn't every day an eighteen-year-old gives a millionaire a crossbar.

Jake and Dave found the London music scene a lot more hectic than Dublin. The first difference was that they had to rehearse more than they had been used to back home in Ireland. Starting a new band wasn't easy, especially when they weren't used to the style and spontaneity of the new drummer and rhythm guitarist. Secondly, more people were involved in the background. Back home, with the exception of Kev's father, they had been totally on their own But currently, in London, there was a team of musical experts helping them to polish up their act. The expertise related not only to musical matters; Jake and Dave were coached in image-building and crowd manipulation, and were even versed in how to handle the media and dodge questions that were too unsavoury to answer.

The most surprising discovery for Jake and Dave was that most of the expertise was coming from people a lot older than themselves, people who in Dublin would be normally regarded as being too long in the tooth to be familiar with the pop scene. But not so in London. Most of the coaching experts were 'well-on', as Jake would say. But they were all dynamic – hard taskmasters and utterly devoted to the job in hand. They would think nothing of gruelling Jake and Dave for five or six hours at a stretch. Not that the other two band members, Mossy on drums and Mike on rhythm guitar, got off much lighter, and they had been around the English professional rock scene a few years longer than the Irish boys.

The record company quickly got the four lads, who luckily got on well enough from the 'off', into a routine.

They were moved into two luxury flats down Chelsea way, Jake and Dave together, Mossy and Mike above them. Mike was a Cockney from the Shepherds Bush area, while Mossy was a rough sort from Manchester's Moss Side. Mossy hated London. Likewise Mike hated Manchester. Oddly enough they got on just fine, their music and humour complementing one another. They were soul brothers.

'Wha' gets you so worked up when you play the drums?'

'I get carried away, that's all. I close me eyes an' imagine I'm floggin' Man Utd supporters.'

Mossy was a Man City fan. A Man City 'True Blue'.

The record company had much more in mind for Jake and Dave than just playing in a rock band. They were interested in their songs.

'This number here'd go down well on a Rod Stewart album.'

'What about us doin' one on our own?' mouthed Jake.

'You're too new to the scene for that. Have to build up a reputation first. A tour of the clubs and see how it goes.'

'And if it doesn't?'

'We'll take the songs. You can write as a team. We'll dish what we're happy with out to established stars.'

'We'll want a contract for that.'

'Sure you'll have a contract, Irish. We all have contracts here – for better or for worse.'

'Well, we'll sign on for a few songs. See how it goes.'

'A few songs?'

'Yeah. We're not goin' to sign our lives away.'

'They're certainly educatin' yous over there nowadays.'

'Sure. There's nothin' else to do.'

'How many songs?'

'Ten.'

'That's not much.'

'With an option for first refusal on the next ten.'

'Who taught you? The Jesuits?'

'As a band we'll contract solely to you.'

'That's considerate. Any further pre-conditions?'

'No, not that I can think of.'

'Good. We'll get the legal documents drawn up.'

'When do we sign the contracts?'

The record company executive paused for a second, a slight smile showing on his face. 'As soon as you learn to sing for your supper.'

Luke got in touch with Mr Creamer, who, true to his word gave him a job. He was to start the following Monday. The tattered combat jacket would have to go. An appointment with the barber was also scheduled Other than that Luke would have to get used to the routine of being up at seven in the morning to catch the bus into Bray and clock into work by eight o'clock. It was a factory job, manufacturing pork products – sausages, pork pies, hams and rashers. Luke had to start at the bottom but Mr Creamer promised him that if he worked hard he would be sent to night-school to study a course in factory management. All things going well he would be eventually introduced to the management side of the business.

Luke wasn't overhappy with the job. But he didn't complain. He knuckled down and did everything that was asked of him. He wasn't a lazy lad, he got stuck in and worked as hard as the best in the factory. What he didn't like about the job was the fact that the sausages, rashers and all the rest were once pigs. He had this thing about animals. And he still had his night-mares.

Two weeks into the job Mr Creamer asked him to transfer to another factory belonging to the company in Mullingar. Luke didn't want to go. He'd be in trouble with his pigeons. He wouldn't be able to look after them.

Luke's father said he'd do it.

'But they need someone to be with them all the time.'

'I'll feed'm before I go to work and when I come home. This isn't the racing season. They won't need much lookin' after. Anyway, you'll be home week-ends.'

'I don't know, Da. It's a bit risky.'

'It's risky not havin' a job. Maybe your boss'll transfer you back to Bray after a few months. See how it goes.'

Reluctantly Luke agreed. He wasn't too fond of the idea of being cut off from his pigeons. The breeding season was imminent.

Monday to Friday, work in Mullingar.

Saturday – Sunday, the utopia of being home in Greystones with his pigeons.

65

7

Lar Holmes and Shamrock Boys were top of the 'D' section of the Dublin Schoolboys League. Riverside, unfortunately, were not in the same happy position. They were in fourth place in the 'B' section, Though they had two matches in hand over the leaders, Mr Glynn couldn't really see them being in contention, as the standard in the 'B' section was very high. Too high for Riverside's liking, with teams like Home Farm B, Leixlip, Lourdes Celtic and St Malachy's in contention. Finish third or fourth and Mr Glynn would be more than happy.

It was obvious that Home Farm B were going to win the League. But as their first team were already in the 'A' section that meant that whoever finished second and third would be promoted at the end of the season. This was because the Dublin Schoolboys League had a rule that no club could have two teams in the same section of the League, so Home Farm B would have to opt out on promotion. From that perspective it wasn't entirely beyond Riverside's capabilities to finish second or third and thus gain promotion to the 'A' section. But for that to happen Mr Glynn and Harry Hennessy knew that the squad needed to be strengthened by the addition of a few more class players. Picking them up would be their top priority.

Some scouting in the Toyota Corolla was a must. As for Riverside's U-14s, they didn't complain, they just let Mr Glynn and Hennessy make the big decisions. The main thing for them was to get on with their football and have a good time.

One of their favourite treats was to watch Harry Hennessy running up and down the sideline red-faced, roaring his heart out.

'He's goin' to burst.'

'Someone gave him rocket-fuel instead of a pint.'

During his refereeing days Harry Hennessy had been a great advantage to Riverside; as a mentor he was a public embarrassment.

'Look at him, roarin' an' shoutin'. He's only makin' a show of us.'

'Where'd he get that track-suit?'

'It ain't a track-suit, it's an Indian wigwam.'

Mr Glynn was much more sedate, more civilized. He hardly ever shouted. Just occasionally motioned. He always saved the verbals for the half-time pep-talk. Not that all the players tuned in. Some would go to the far side of the trees on the side-line and have a quick smoke. But Mr Glynn was very good with the half-time refreshments. He always laid on three large bottles of minerals: Fanta, Coke and Seven-Up.

'Giv's a slug.'

'You got enough. Giv's the bottle.'

'I ain't finished. One more slug.'

Then the pushing and shoving would start.

'Mr Glynn, I got none. Slugger Sullivan wouldn't give me none.'

'You wouldn't give me a smoke.'

'I only had a butt.'

'You coulda given me a drag.'

'Here's the bottle then,'

'It's empty.'

All three bottles were empty. Fanta, Coke, Seven-Up, all gone. But Slugger Sullivan had a bottle with him. It was at his feet, right next to the tree. It was full, full of Holy Water. His mother had told him to bring it around to his granny after the match. Harry Hennessy, with a terrible thirst, caught sight of the bottle. It looked tempting. He lowered the contents in one gulp and handed the bottle back to Slugger.

'Thanks.'

Slugger and Bonkers O'Toole looked at one another in disgust.

'See that?'

'Yeah, he knocked back t'whole bottle o' Holy Water.'

'He's worse than an alcoholic... What's worse than an alcoholic?'

'Don't know.'

Harry had gone off down the touchline, indifferent to the stares and resentment. Whatever about being an alcoholic, there was one thing Harry certainly wasn't – Dracula!

While Harry Hennessy was making a show of Riverside, Lar Holmes was having something of a similar effect on Shamrock Boys' image. Though his quirk was with the officials of the Dublin Schoolboys League, mainly ringing up and telling them that Gavin's brother, Garry, should be included on the Dublin Schoolboys U-14 Kennedy Cup panel.

'Who's that?'

'Its me, Lar Holmes.'

'What's it this time?'

'You should definitely reconsider Garry Byrne for the Kennedy Cup squad.'

'He hasn't got the power... the pace.'

'Rubbish. He was brilliant last Saturday. You should have seen him.'

'We have, twice.'

'He scored a hat-trick, three gems.'

'He hasn't got the physique.'

There was a clicking sound. The Dublin Schoolboys official had hung-up.

Lar fumed. In his opinion the League didn't know a good player when they saw one. Still, he'd champion Garry Byrne's inclusion to the bitter end.

Over the following few weeks the U-14 League management got totally fed-up with Lar phoning in. He kept going on about Garry Byrne. He had become a proper pain in the neck.

'That lad from Greystones is on the phone again.'

'Lar Holmes?'

'Yeah. He wants to talk to you.'

'Tell him I'm not here. Did you give him my home number?'

'No.'

'Thank God for that.'

Garry Byrne was unlikely to make the Dublin & District Schoolboys League Kennedy Cup squad.

The weather was damp and cold. Sam Gregson had the reserves out on Highfield's wide open spaces for over an hour-and-a-half, going through a strenuous training routine. There had been some backstabbing the day before. Two of the senior players on the reserves, Andy Higgins and Clive Turner, had made a few out-of-order remarks, sparked off not only by the fact that they had lost their last three games, but by the sure knowledge that both of them had fallen out of favour and were unlikely to make it back into first-team football and the glamour of the Premiership.

'Sam ain't got the bottle to make firm decisions no more. He's dodgin' the issues,' remarked Andy Higgins.

'Don't tell me. Say it to his face.'

And Andy did, at the first opportunity.

'Sam, you're all washed-up.'

'Say that again?'

'You're past it. Don't know how to pick a team no more. You're lettin' Stuart Clement pick the team.'

'Stuart Clements is a player. As manager I pick the team, no one else. No one else, hear me?'

'That's not the way the rest of us see it…'

'What do y' mean, the rest of us?'

'The squad.'

'Yourself and Clive Turner. It's not me that's washed

out. It's you two. Don't dare undermine my authority.'

'Sam, you ain't got no authority. You lost it all up North.'

Sam Gregson was taken aback. The comment brought him back sharply to the end of his days in the North of England, when his confidence had been sapped by hostile media attention. Outwardly he didn't let it show, but he had suffered. His family had suffered. Now that he was back in football he knew his future at London Albion depended on making a stand. That was why, instead of the usual five-a-side and the tactical discussions, he ordered a trek of cross-country running.

The team trainer supervised the lap order. Once... twice ... three times, four ... five ... six times, the laps, each at least a mile-and-a-half, went by. At the end of the sixth lap Sam halted the squad beside a mud-patch. He got the players to run up and down through the mud time after time. To Sam the mud-patch wasn't intended as a test of the players' stamina, but as a demonstration of his own authority.

It wasn't long before the two rabble-rousers from the previous day acted up.

'We ain't doin' any more of that.'

'Do it, or else...'

'Or else, what?'

Andy Higgins and Clive Turner felt smug. Sam Gregson was a spent force. They'd walk all over him.

'Do it!'

Andy and Clive didn't give a damn, they just laughed at Sam.

Sam called Hammer's name – told him to run through the mud.

The two rebel players tried to block him but he did as Sam Gregson requested.

Then Mick Bates was called, and so right through the squad. Each player responded and ran through the mud. They all understood what was at stake: not just Sam

Gregson's authority, but his self-esteem.

Andy Higgins and Clive Turner were called last. But Sam's order fell on deaf ears. Defiant to the end, they were told to report to John Warner.

'Why him? Haven't you got the bottle to discipline us yourself?'

Sam was terse: 'I'm not club manager. John Warner's that. But I'll be recommending that both of you are put on the transfer list. That's all I can do. Maybe then we'll win a few matches.'

The two players weren't expecting John Warner to be introduced to the saga. They knew they would be in trouble.

And they were. John Warner rapidly got rid of them.

'Where's the last of our signing-on fee, boss?'

'Signing-on fee? You mean loyalty fee.'

'Yeah, loyalty fee. Call it what you like.'

'You term causing trouble being loyal?'

'We ain't caused no trouble, boss.'

'Ever since you've been dropped from the first-team squad the pair of you have caused nothing but trouble. There's no loyalty fee in your instance. You've broken the terms of your contracts. And if you think you can drive a wedge between me and Sam Gregson – even Ted Brinsley for that matter – you won't. Sam Gregson has done more for the good of football at every club he's been at. I won't allow two-bit snakes in the grass like yourselves to undermine him. You're getting no loyalty payments, no nothing, until some unfortunate club comes in for you. Both of you are suspended without pay.'

'Without pay?'

'Yes, without pay.'

'You can't do that.'

'I can. It's written in the small print of your contracts. Get your glasses and have a squint.'

'Ted Brinsley's out to replace you with Sam Gregson.'

'Only if I leave the club. And I'm not leaving. Get out!'

Exit the two dissidents. Some day soon they would be another club's problem. But the issue involving the pair brought something to his mind. He summoned Sam Gregson to his office. 'What I'm going to say is confidential, just between you and me. Sam, I've been talking to Ted Brinsley. A few things have cropped up lately, a few things I don't like. Ted is, as you know, big in the insurance business. His company's branching out into real estate. They're setting up a subsidiary. Well, they're launching a scheme to attract investors to the company – a venture capital fund, he calls it. Whatever investors come in have an assurance that their money will be safe in the new company. So to placate any fears they might have Ted has agreed to sell his shares in the company at a cut-price rate in the event of anything going wrong.'

'What's that got to do with football?'

'On the face of it, nothing really. But in reality a lot. You see, it's a bit complicated, but I'll try to explain. There are two points. Point one: Ted Brinsley is by far the major shareholder in London Albion. He has huge influence in the boardroom. He always gets his way. Point two: only for Ted Brinsley this club would be broke. He pumps the money in. Also on point two: with this new real-estate set-up, most of Ted's spare money would be going into that to keep the share-value up until the business is well established. That means there'll be very little of Ted's money coming into London Albion. And we need money, lots of it right now. So where's the money going to come from? Only one place. Players will have to be sold. Ted's been on to me already. He's got the itch.'

'How many players?'

'Two at the start of next season – Mel Thorpe and Dwight Crawford. But there's more. Part of it's my fault. A few weeks ago Aston Villa were on to me for Gavin Byrne. They offered £900,000. I told Ted Brinsley, afraid the Villa would try and do a deal behind my back. Ted was delighted. He told me to get Gavin Byrne on to the first team before the end of the season, and all going well we'd flog him off to the highest bidder before the end of next season. To lose Mel and Dwight Crawford is bad enough. But to lose Gavin, that's the end.

'I've said nothing to Ted, but I'm not signing another contract for London Albion. I'm going up North, near enough to your old stomping ground. Liverpool want me. Come next season I'm gone. I don't know how you're feeling about all this, but London Albion will have to go through a transition period. How they come out the other side I don't know. It'll be a sticky wicket to manage. Are you still interested in the job?'

'Beggars can't be choosers. It's my only chance. What else have I got?'

'At least you'll be going in with your eyes open... But London Albion could have another long-term problem. Ted owns two-thirds of the shares and is well capable of buying out the others if he wanted, Now there's this new subsidiary of his – real estate.

'Maybe I have a bad mind, but some day he could be tempted to sell the grounds off and move the club elsewhere and so improve his bank balance. It's happened before.'

'Doesn't leave London Albion on very firm ground, does it?'

'No, but Ted has put a lot of money into London Albion in the past and he loves the club. I only hope somewhere along the line he doesn't grow to love money more ... Don't repeat any of this to anyone.'

'Certainly not. Most of it's speculation anyway, isn't it?'

'Hopefully. But selling off players? There's no future for me here. Ted Brinsley won't have my signature on a new contract. End of season I'm gone.'

'No hard feelings?'

'Not against you. I had no intention of leaving Albion, not until all this cropped up. There's plenty of good young players coming through. Pity is, Ted has his eyes on who to sell. You'll have a good backroom staff already in place. You'll have the best scouting system going, bar none. What's more, Stevie Hodgson and Bill Thornbull are doing a great job with the Youths. Everything won't be a downer, there's a lot of pluses.'

'Thanks, John, for the way you handled Andy Higgins and Clive Turner.'

'No sweat... There's one other thing, Gavin Byrne's contract is down for renewal next August. I'll get him to sign another before then. That way, it would suit the club best. Talking of Gavin, how's Shane Teale coming on?'

'There was a confidence problem. It's sorted out now. He's doing just fine.'

'Funny about Hammer. I signed him more to counteract Gavin getting homesick. His contract is also due up the start of next season. Would he have a place in your plans?'

'He's worth keeping for the time being. If players are going to be sold off he may be needed soon enough.'

'Good kid. Safe as a house. There's not much between him and Cyril Stevens. Pity Ted Brinsley's out there putting a spanner in the works. But we can't complain. Money talks, it's what keeps the professional game alive. I suppose what our game is really about is surviving, not winning, much as the fans and sport columnists like to think otherwise.'

Surviving but not winning. Surviving and winning, that was the perfect combination. But sometimes winners didn't survive. John Warner was right. Surviving was the most important be-all of professional football.

Sam Gregson left John Warner's office a lot happier than when he came in. John Warner had put his mind at rest. Next season he'd be back at the top of the managerial ladder. If that wasn't enough to boost his ego nothing was.

Come next season, circumstance would have turned full-circle. Thanks to Ted Brinsley's meddling he would be back in the big-time again.

A few weeks later a call came through to Highfield for Gavin and Hammer. Luckily, Hammer was in the pavilion at the time. The call was from Elaine in Turin. She didn't sound too happy.

'What's the matter, Elaine?'

'I've had some bad luck. I damaged the cruciate ligaments in my knee.'

'What the hell are cru... oui... ligaments?'

'Something serious if you pick up an injury. They had to operate.'

'Sorry, Elaine, that's bad. Will everything be all right?'

'I hope so. Is Gavin there?'

'He's outside training. I'll pass the message on.'

'How are things with both of you?'

'Pretty good. Gavin's on the verge of makin' the first team. Me, I'm still in there with a fightin' chance. Everything's fine. Sorry to hear about your injury.'

'It's getting me down. Everything was going so well, and then... Juventus had a top surgeon perform the operation. He says I'll be all right. A year, and hopefully the knee will be okay again.'

'Will you come home for Christmas?'

'Maybe for a while. Juventus want me here in Turin for treatment and some exercise to build up the knee again. Say hello to Gavin for me.'

'Okay.'

'Good-bye.'

'See you, Elaine.'

Elaine had damaged her knee a few weeks earlier in an important top-of-the-table clash at home to arch rivals Milan. The game was watched by 20,000 fanatical supporters. Dariusz Kowalczyk gave Elaine a roving role, hoping that she would unlock the Milan 'Libero' defensive system, and perhaps leave the Juventus star forward, Anna Radice, with a few much needed goal-scoring opportunities.

Anna wasn't the only star performer on the Juventus team. Maria Borgonovo, a defensive midfielder, was an Italian international, as was Francesca Silenzi, the left-full, and the defensive partnership of Maria Malusci and Isabella Pusceddu. They had one other international, Collette Geerts, who played for Belgium.

Another star was Maria Francini, lethal from twenty to twenty-five yards, a top notch free-taker. In the Italian world of football she was the female equivalent of Roberto Baggio when it came to taking free kicks. It was some coincidence that both played for the same club – Juventus.

'Juve! Juve! Juve!'

'Milano! Milano! Milano!'

'Maria Francini!'

The Juventus supporters were in fine fettle, as were Milan's banner-carrying aficionados.

A ticker-tape of shredded paper flitted from the highest vantage points of the stands. Gaily coloured banners fluttered all around the ground. The stadium was a crescendo of chants, claxtons, banners and flares as the two teams walked from the tunnel. Elaine was fifth in line as the team walked out, wearing the Number 7 that she had worn ever since her schoolgirl days. Cameras flashed as the press followed the teams across the pitch.

Another roar of appreciation erupted from the crowd.

Then a Juve chant, 'Radice! Radice! Radice!'

The two teams knocked practice balls about, did a few warm-up exercises, took off their tracksuit tops.

'Juve!'

'Milano!'

The referee called the two captains together. The toss. Change of ends.

'Chichi!'

Elaine turned and acknowledged the chant of a section of the Juventus fans.

'Chichi!'

The practice balls were kicked in the general direction of the dug-outs. The match ball was placed on the centre-circle. The referee checked his watch, waited for the precise kick-off time – blew his whistle – the ball was centred and the game was on.

Juventus got into their stride straightway. Anna Radice was sent sprawling outside the Milan penalty area. Collette Geerts stepped forward to take the free kick. Milan formed a wall. Their Number 8 had to be warned by the referee to put ten yards between herself and the place where the free kick was being taken. She withdrew. Maria Francini, instead of Collette Geerts, took the free. She sent a curving shot for the top corner. The ball clipped the bar and spun on to the roof of the net.

Attack followed attack.

Milan settled, but not enough to stem the flow of the Juve threat.

After thirty-four minutes Juventus scored the first goal of the game. Elaine took the ball from Maria Borgonovo out wide on the right. She beat a Milan player. Then another. A third Milan player shaped up to tackle her. Elaine swerved and played a precision pass to Anna Radice who took the ball first time and angled a shot between the goalkeeper and the far post. The ball squeezed just inside the upright.

Juventus 1– Milan 0

Halfway through the second half the score was still 1–0 in favour of Juventus. Elaine ran on to a through-ball from Isabella Pusceddu. Clatter! Rolled to the ground in agony from a Milan tackle and the Juventus crowd cat-called in anger. The offending player received a warning and Juventus were awarded a free kick. But Elaine was still on the ground. Her knee hurt like hell. The crowd hushed as a stretcher was called for. They feared the worst. Elaine was put on the stretcher.

The Juventus crowd started up a chant, 'Chichi! Chichi!'

Elaine was in real trouble. She almost passed out with the pain.

Next thing she was in the first-aid room looking up at the bright white of the ceiling, clutching in agony the sides of the stretcher. The Juventus doctor examined her knee. It took him only a matter of seconds to diagnose the trouble. He called the attendants. Straightway she was brought to a parking bay directly across from the first-aid room, where there was an ambulance on stand-by. She was lifted on the stretcher and put into the back of the ambulance. All she was aware of was the pain, which if anything was getting worse. She was not conscious of the hovering attendant or the sharp whirr of the siren as they sped through the crowded Turin streets.

Within five minutes she was in the casualty department of one of Turin's most exclusive hospitals. She was brought to the X-ray unit where her damaged knee was X-rayed. She was then taken up to a private suite where she was made comfortable. Within minutes of the X-rays being examined a hurried discussion took place. An emergency call went out for one of the hospital's top surgeons to get to the hospital as quickly as possible. Elaine's knee would have to be operated on. Whether the operation would be successful was problematic but it was essential that it be performed at once. Her entire future lay in the hands of the surgeon.

Elaine didn't wake up until night-time. The operation was over. Her complete leg was in plaster, her foot in traction. She felt groggy and sore – and frightened. Then a nurse came in. She reassured her, told her not to worry, and said the surgeon would be in to see her in the morning. Elaine asked for pain-killers and a glass of water. Her knee still hurt like mad. The nurse gave her the pain-killers and within five minutes she was sound asleep.

Elaine was awake when the surgeon came into the room.

Wide awake. The surgeon was a tall, thin man. The morning was dull. Through the window Elaine could see a patch of grey sky.

'How are you?'

'Not too bad.'

'The news isn't good, I'm afraid.'

'How bad?'

'There's a possibility you'll never be able to play professional football again.'

'How do you know?'

The surgeon had the X-rays of Elaine's knee with him. He showed them, before and after the operation, with and without the synthetic plastic ligament that was placed in the knee during the operation. 'You'll have to get a lot of physiotherapy during you recovery period. First the joint will have to be rested. That will cause other problems, as the rest period will weaken your thigh muscles. Everything will have to be built up again from scratch. It will take a huge effort on your part. We tried to save the original ligament by stapling it back on to the bone but the damage was too severe. Only time will tell whether or not you can play again. Most players who suffer such an injury don't make it back. You should be prepared for the worst.'

'What's the worst?'

'You'll never play football again.'

'At any level?'

'Yes, your football days could be over.'

Elaine felt crushed. She looked towards the window. A darkness was creeping into the grey patch of cloud outside.

Already she knew the surgeon would be going back to his rooms and drawing up a report for the insurance company and the club's accountants. Elaine had heard of it happening – players getting crocked and being paid off. Her club hadn't been in touch yet, but they would, probably with an insurance claim form in one hand and a pen in the other for her to add her signature. She felt cynical, depressingly so. But one thing was sure, she was going to fight back. She would prove the surgeon wrong. She wouldn't quit.

The surgeon was gone now, back to his office or surgery or whatever. Elaine looked out of the window again. Outside the grey patch was gone. All of a sudden she felt isolated and alone.

But there was no need to be totally depressed, not so far as Juventus was concerned. Most of the players were in to see her that night. Anna Radice, Isabella Pusceddu and Collette Geerts brought beautiful floral bouquets. Dariusz Kowalczyk came in too, and some of the club's top officials. There were also lots of get-well cards and bouquets from the fans. Elaine appreciated all the attention. At least, she wasn't forgotten about.

Just before visiting hours began, she made a phone-call to her parents. When her father heard she had damaged her cruciate ligaments he was prepared for the worst. He had seen too many old pros having to give up over the same injury. Though in terms of medical progress in the treatment of football injuries all wasn't doom and gloom, privately he didn't hold out much hope. He could only pray that everything would be all right – that she would be able to play football again.

8

Early in December Gavin was called into the first-team squad. The fixture was an away Coca-Cola Cup tie to Huddersfield. He couldn't believe his luck, although the signs were already obvious, as he was being occasionally asked to train with the first team. John Warner had taken him to one side on the morning of the match and told Gavin he was a late addition to the travelling party. That more than likely he would be one of the listed substitutes.

Hammer, when he got word, wanted to go up from London on the first-team coach but John Warner wouldn't allow it.

'I want to be there in case Gavin gets a game.'

'Get a train. Get a bus. But you aren't travelling on the first-team coach.'

Hammer looked doleful. He was afraid to go on his own. An overnight stay would be involved. Huddersfield! It would be like going to the moon, it was that far away. Middle of winter. If the weather suddenly changed he could get stranded. Reluctantly, he gave Gavin's hoped for introduction to first-team football a miss and stayed put in London. He watched a re-run of an old Bruce Lee film on TV: *Enter the Dragon*. When they were younger Jake used to call it *Enter the Flagon*.

He didn't blame John Warner for not allowing him to travel on the first-team coach. If he had, a precedence would have been set. Every apprentice and Youth in the club would abuse the privilege to travel the length and breadth of the country to watch top-class soccer for free. No, if you travelled on the first-team coach you had to be a first-team player.

Coincidently, after the coach left for Huddersfield

Hammer went down Chelsea way to tell Jake about the match. He was only wasting his time. A neighbour said Jake and the band were gone since early morning to do a gig in Newcastle. They were staying overnight and wouldn't be back until tea-time the following day. Jake would miss the match. He'd be furious. Anyway, maybe it was all for the better, Jake had a habit of getting over-excited at football matches.

For Gavin, the match against Huddersfield was a big occasion – a milestone in his life. On the coach-trip up from London John Warner promised him a run-out during the course of the game. Some of the top sports correspondents would be present. Not just some local hopscotch reporters, but some of the top soccer hacks in the country. Reporters could make, or obliterate, a reputation at the stroke of a pen. What was about to happen in Huddersfield wasn't the South-East Counties League; it was big-time football in the raw.

Huddersfield: it wasn't a place a traveller would particularly remember; then again it wasn't a place that would be quickly forgotten.

'Harold Wilson supported Huddersfield in his younger days.'

'Who's Harold Wilson?'

'A man who smoked a pipe.'

Some place Huddersfield! The team coach took hours to get there. Driving into town in the coach the place looked dreary. When they got to the stadium, out on the Leeds road, the evening light was rapidly fading. In the half-light they could distinguish the outline of a field behind one of the goals. The field sloped upward, almost perpendicularly to the stadium wall behind the goal. A snowfall, and the field would have done justice to an Olympic ski-slope.

The London Albion squad had a short walk around the pitch, studying the terrain. Then they went back into town to one of Huddersfield's top hotels for a light meal and to unwind after the coach journey. Then it was back to Leeds Road to confront Huddersfield Town and go about eliminating them from the Coca-Cola Cup.

The stadium was nice and compact, with a very homely atmosphere. That was before kick-off time though. When the place filled up the atmosphere changed into a typical Yorkshire frenzy of football passion. It was odds on Huddersfield would never see the glory days again, days when a young Denis Law donned the famous blue and white, days when players like Trevor Cherry and Frank Worthington were stars of the First Division for Huddersfield.

Even though Gavin was only a sub, walking out before ten thousand Huddersfield fans really boosted his morale. As soon as he set foot on the pitch for the pre-match kick-about he was really drawn into the atmosphere set by the crowd. The 'Town Terriers' were in full flow. He felt nervous, though it was always good to feel slightly keyed-up; it kept the adrenalin going. He didn't mind being only a listed substitute, and couldn't have cared less that he'd be sitting on the bench, half freezing, waiting for a last fifteen-minutes call to action. The important thing was that he was part of the scene, on the threshold of making his first-team debut. What was more, he knew John Warner had every confidence in his ability. That the experts, with prior inside information, regarded him as London Albion's new star, the best player to come across the Irish sea in thirty years, George Best excluded.

Mick Bates was in the line-up, as was Dwight Crawford.

For the first twenty minutes Huddersfield gave as good as they got. They closed down the Albion midfield, didn't give them time on the ball, set up a few incisive moves of their own.

Gradually, Mick Bates began to make his mark. He began to win a lot of ball. Laid a few passes on for Dwight Crawford to take the pressure off the defence. Just to add some variation a few long balls were played through the middle for Chris Morgan, the 'Albinos' centre-forward to run on to. He rounded the Huddersfield centre-half twice, only for the ball to be deflected out of play by the Huddersfield goalkeeper. He was on the verge of rounding the centre-half a third time when the centre-half clattered him. Insofar as Chris Morgan was concerned it was a costly tackle. It left him limping. Five minutes later he had to be substituted. Gavin came on in his place.

By now Huddersfield's midfield had flagged; London Albion were winning a lot of possession. Gavin blended in straightway.

'Give's the ball!'

The Huddersfield centre-half lined up Gavin in his sights and fouled him.

Direct free.

The ball skimmed the edge of the Huddersfield goal-post, and bounced back into play off an advertisement hoarding.

The goalkeeper grabbed hold of it, placed it on the edge of the six-yard box and launched a huge punt downfield.

'Town!' 'Town!'

The crowd was doing its utmost to lift the team's spirit. Huddersfield were on a bad run lately, and it was beginning to show. After the first twenty minutes they quickly lost their momentum. They couldn't compete with Dwight Crawford and Mick Bates in midfield. For his part, Gavin had quickly come to grips with the centre-half. He suffered no more clatterings. Gavin was too wily. The centre-half just couldn't make contact.

Dwight Crawford moved to take a throw-in. He edged down the line.

A woman's voice croaked behind him, 'Crawford, you big-headed twit!'

Dwight turned and roared back, 'Nora Batty, how's your knickers?' The referee cautioned him, took his name and told him to belt up.

Dwight took it all in his stride and got on with the game.

Half-an-hour into the game Huddersfield were beginning to feel the pace. Tony Jenkins, the London Albion left-full, sprinted down the flank only to be fouled by a Huddersfield defender. He took the free himself. Played it back to Mel Thorpe, a full English international. Mel jinked through the middle and split the Huddersfield defence wide open. He drew the keeper, stroked the ball to the keeper's left, but the goalkeeper got a touch and the ball was deflected to Gavin. He calmly cut inside a covering defender and first-timed the ball into the empty net.

Huddersfield 0 London Albion 1

As soon as the ball hit the back of the net Gavin turned and raised a pointed finger in the air. To the old-timers in the stand Gavin's gesture brought back memories of a young Denis Law. Denis Law always pointed his finger in the air after he scored a goal. There was the same instant reaction with Gavin. Only that his hair was red the old-timers could have sworn they were looking at the young Denis Law. They took more notice of Gavin after that and watched his every move. They were entranced. And when Gavin scored his second goal on the stroke of half-time with a quick reflex touch of the ball, and when the finger nonchantly pointed skywards again, and when that impish smile came to his face, they were convinced they were looking at the new Denis Law.

In the second half, the game turned into a cake-walk for London Albion, although the amount of possession didn't translate on to the scoreboard. Albion only scored one further goal, headed in off a corner by Scotch Pete, the Albion's centre-half. The game was over bar the shouting. The second leg, at Brompton, would be a mere formality. Lying mid-table in the Premiership, John Warner was convinced the team could go all the way to Wembley.

As the team coach cruised smoothly back to London John Warner turned to Sam Gregson and said, 'Glad you came?'

'Sure.'

'Hopefully it'll be a sign of the times when you run the show next season.'

'If Ted Brinsley doesn't sell off all the best players.'

'You'll manage, Next season's your year. Huddersfield's your watershed. Remember Huddersfield.'

'Yeah, I'll remember Huddersfield.'

Gavin would also remember Huddersfield. He sat contentedly staring into the darkness outside the coach window as it sped along the motorway.

John Warner came over to him. 'You'll be in for the League game against Notts Forest mid-January. Don't forget to let your folks know.'

Gavin let out a roar of delight.

Behind him, Dwight Crawford was intent on reading something he was trying hard to keep under wraps.

'What's that, Dwight? *Playboy?*'

'No, *National Geographic*.'

Gavin wasn't interested. He was dreaming about a Saturday early in January.

Dwight snuggled back into the magazine, only it wasn't the National Geographic. It was *The Beano!*

About the time Albion were arriving back in London Jake was finishing gigging in Newcastle. They had gone North on their own, though everything had been prearranged, and had driven around Newcastle in their newly acquired Mercedes-Benz bandwagon looking for the night-club they were booked to play at.

Jeff Cooper, the Cockney driver of the bandwagon, didn't seem to have a clue where he was going.

'I thought you knew Newcastle inside out, Jeff.'

'I did, until they changed things.'

'By the look of the place there's not much to change.'

'They can change the names of the clubs, can't they? They're always changin' names up here. Don't know where they're 'arf the time.'

'What's the name of the club?'

' 'Untingdale's, I think.'

'Sure? Doesn't sound like the name of a night-club to me. Sounds more like a farmyard. There's a fella over there, ask 'im.'

'Ey, mate, where's 'Untingdale's?'

The Geordie kindly gave directions, consisting of a maze of right turns, with two lefts thrown in, plus a few street names. The lads hadn't a clue what he was saying.

'Could you write that down?' asked Jeff.

'He'd get writers' cramp writin' that lot down. We'll find it for ourselves.'

Half-an-hour later they found the club.

It wasn't the most pleasant of places. It was more like an underground cavern. To be charitable, it lacked class.

'You'd have a job gettin' electrocuted in this place.'

The manager asked them if they would like something to eat.

'Yes, please.'

He sent them around the corner to a stand-up fish and chip shop; the name was The Three Musketeers. In keeping with tradition there were only three items on the menu: fresh cod, chips and cans of Coke.

'Give us five rounds of everythin', only don't wrap it up. We aim to eat it, not hoard it.'

The proprietor duly obliged. The fresh cod, newly smuggled in from Grimsby, was delicious.

Then it was back to the club. Two hours later it was full to capacity. Jake, Dave, Mike and Mossy weren't asking any questions. They just wanted to get on with the gig, get it over with and get out of the place as quickly as possible. A local band acted as support group, to get the crowd going. By the time Tin Knights (Jake and company) came on the crowd was on an absolute high. Tin Knights gave it their best shot. The place went mad. Three hours of raw emotion. By the time it was all over they just had enough energy left to run from the stage and barricade themselves into the dressing-rooms. The female fraternity were running riot. They had taken a fancy to Tin Knights. An hour later it was safe to come out.

'Was that for real?' groaned Jake.

'It was for real all right,' smiled the club owner. 'You fellas really went down a bomb. There wouldn't be much of yous left if yous played here every week. Want to come back?'

'Maybe. You can pay us for the gig now.'

"Fraid not. The place was robbed while yous were on stage. I'll send the money down to London soon as I can.'

'We'd like to be paid now.'

'You Irish?'

'Yes, so what?'

'Nothin'. Sorry, lads. Yous juss 'ave to take my word. The money's all gone. There's nothin' I can do.'

'We've got people like you back in Ireland. Know what they're called?'

'No, what?'

'Bishops.'

The night-club proprietor didn't see the connection. He was an Anglican.

'Any chance of givin' us the petrol money back to London?'

'Sure, that'll come out of petty cash.'

'You're supposed to put us up for the night.'

'Sure, Harry-O'll look after that.'

'Who's Harry-O?'

'He's one of the bouncers.'

It didn't sound promising. Harry-O hardly owned a luxury hotel. When they saw the cut of him they wondered if he even owned a house.

It was three o'clock by the time they got the band equipment loaded up. Then Harry-O took them back to his house. He had a spare room with a double bed. The sleeping arrangements were: two at each end, with Jeff, the bandwagon driver, sleeping in a corner of the room on some cushions. There was a lovely settee downstairs but Harry-O would't let any of them sleep there for fear it would upset his cat.

At half-past-nine that morning they were up and ready, back on the road, experiencing the luxury of the long haul to London. Life in the fast lane wasn't quite what it was cracked up to be.

Luke wasn't feeling any better; the nightmares persisted. He wasn't settling into his job either. It wasn't so much Mullingar – it was quite a nice place and the people were pleasant – or being away from home. It was the factory which was really beginning to unnerve him. He could only wish and hope that he would be moved back to Bray and off the factory floor altogether.

After all, Mr Creamer had said he was going to send him to night-school; that if he studied hard he would consider putting him on a management training course. But Creamer was proving to be the proverbial 'Will-o-the-Wisp'. Since he had left Bray Luke hadn't heard from, nor seen the man. He had this feeling he'd be stuck in the Mullingar factory for the rest of his life. True, he could have walked out of the job, but he'd have his father to answer to. Jobs were hard to come by. He wondered if he should ask the factory manager to get in touch with Mr Creamer? Maybe he could explain his case that way. But the factory manager would have none of it. There was no point in wasting the boss's time. He'd be in touch when it suited him.

Already Luke's mind was beginning to play tricks. He detested the factory; the row upon row of boned meat; the cold storage facilities; the slaughter-house across the yard.

The slaughter-yard was a constant threat, an habitual nightmare. That was really at the heart of the problem – he couldn't stop thinking about animals getting slaughtered. The thought was with him day and night, screaming inside his head, tearing at his conscience.

Once, in Bray, when he was down at the harbour looping pigeons, he glimpsed something floating up-river in the Dargle. As it came closer he saw that it was a cow. There was a slaughter-yard about two hundred yards upstream. The cow had probably smelt the blood and blindly bolted into the river. It literally swam past Luke into the basin of the harbour. It had a look of terror in its eyes that he would never forget.

Some of the men from the slaughter-yard had followed it downstream. They stood on the quay with ropes and looped poles, but the cow was too far out from the pier for their equipment to be effective. Some of the harbour fishermen had come over and discussed going out in boats and trying too drive the cow in against the pier. But while they were talking the cow swam from the harbour into the open sea.

A squad-car arrived. It left the quayside and tracked the cow as it swam parallel with the Promenade towards Bray Head. Luke got on his bike and followed in pursuit. The cow staggered ashore at an inlet called the Cove. Seemingly, the Gardai had rung for a vet. When he arrived Luke watched from a bank overlooking the Cove. The vet had something that looked like a rifle. He went up to the cow and shot it through the head.

For Luke, the episode had a very upsetting effect, and working around the slaughter-house just wasn't the place to be. He wanted to see Mr Creamer badly. He even rang the number he had been given up on the Cliff Walk. But he wasn't there. Mr Creamer was no longer available.

After her cruciate ligament operation, Elaine was in plaster for six weeks and had to use crutches for a further four weeks. She would need physiotherapy, and then the hard gruelling slog would begin to build up her wasted thigh muscles and get herself fit again. It was a very trying period for her. She felt at an all-time low, sitting in her high-rise apartment, the cramped Turin skyline reducing her to breaking point.

She wanted to go home to Greystones for a few weeks' holiday to break the monotony but Juventus wouldn't hear of it. They preferred her to stay in Turin, close at hand, for fear if she went home she wouldn't want to come back. Elaine was Juventus property now and she had to do as they dictated.

So she stuck it out, feeling that if she could endure the next few weeks she could endure anything.

Her only consolation was a few phone-calls home.

'Hang-on in there,' her father told her. 'It's not like the old days, cruciate ligament operations are relatively straightforward now. It's just a long healing process and struggle to get fit again.'

The old days! The legendary Brian Clough's career had been destroyed by a cruciate ligament injury. But that was the old days. Ligament surgery was much more advanced nowadays. Gazza had survived a cruciate ligament injury. So had Alan Shearer. So too could Elaine. But it was the aimless sitting around that annoyed her. One thing, though: she wouldn't allow herself to get fat on pasta.

Though Dariusz Kowalczyk and the girls on the team were very good to her, deep down it just didn't cut ice. What she really needed around her at that point in time was her family. That she resisted temptation and didn't make a break for home, with the airport only half a mile away, was greatly to her credit. But Elaine had gumption. She had come to Italy to make it as a professional footballer. She wasn't going to wilt and run for home.

She had only one doubt. Would the operation be a success? Would she be as good as before the injury?

Only time would tell.

During the first week of December Bray was a hive of activity. As usual, the Main Street was choked with traffic, the shops thronged with shoppers, and the Chamber of Commerce had workers putting up the Christmas lights. There was a stir about the town; the pre-Christmas shopping spree had begun.

The shoppers weren't the only element causing a stir that particular week. Lar Holmes, Sean Dunlop and Eddie Reilly were on patrol in their Wicklow County Council truck. They were in the Vevay, passing time, when a call came through for them to go to the Quinsboro Road. There was a reported water-burst. A mains pipe was fractured. To repair it, the road would have to be dug up. Lar and company sent word to Kilpedder to the County Council Depot for a compressor to be sent in to Bray. But before it arrived a Bray Urban Council truck came on the scene. It had a compressor in tow.

'What are yous doin' here?' asked Lar Holmes suspiciously.

'We came to fix the burst.'

'What burst?'

'The one that's showerin' down on top of yous.'

'This is our burst, not yours.'

'Get off it, Lar. You've no compressor, no drills. You'll hold up the traffic. Let's in, we'll fix it.'

'No. This is a mains burst. Wicklow County Council look after mains bursts.'

Lar was adamant. So too were Sean Dunlop and Eddie Reilly. Meanwhile the traffic was piling up all the way back around the corner, down into Little Bray, out past the roundabout, on to both the road for Shankill and the by-pass.

The Gardai arrived, but there was very little they could do. The two Council crews were totally at loggerheads, standing in their wet gear, glistening in the spray of the water-burst.

The Town Engineer arrived. He tried to coerce Lar and

company into letting the Bray crew repair the burst.

'This calls for the union. We're callin' the union in if you interfere. It's nothin' to do with you. It's a County job... Ring the County Manager,' ranted Lar.

Just then, a lightly-built Wicklow County Council worker came timidly down the Quinsboro Road. 'We got the compressor, Lar. But we're stuck in traffic way up past the Town Hall. The whole place is a bottle-neck. We can't move.'

What he had said was quite correct. Every main traffic artery in the centre of the town was totally blocked by a mass of stationary cars unable to move clear of the locale. What was more, with the Quinsboro Road being on a level surface, water from the burst main was beginning to flow into some of the shops.

It was obvious Lar, Sean and Eddie were going to defy the Bray crew and the Town Engineer, even the Gardai, to the bitter end.

'What are you going to dig the road up with?' shouted the Town Engineer.

'We got pick-axes. We'll use them.'

'Pick-axes! You'll be all week. This is not on! It's just not on!'

All week? By the end of the day the traffic would be halfway to Dublin and Wicklow respectively.

'I can't believe this.'

'You'd better.'

The Town Engineer had had enough. He had a quick word with the Gardai. Reinforcements were called for and just as Lar, Sean and Eddie were warming up with their pick-axes they were grabbed and frog-marched through the traffic to the Gardai barracks and held in custody until the Bray crew finished repairing the fractured pipe.

'I want a solicitor. I demand representation!' roared Lar.

'Give over, Lar,' said Eddie Reilly, 'and ask that copper there for three nice mugs of tea. Sure they'll only keep us for a few hours and then we can go home. It beats workin' in the muck. Let them sodden Bray lads suffer.'

Lar was unrepentant, so the Gardai took the easy way out and locked him up in a cell.

Sean and Eddie weren't too put out by the fact that Lar was locked up. They knew that the incarceration was only a cooling process. Once he tired of roaring he'd be released. That wouldn't be too long – only a few hours and the three of them could reclaim the truck, that's if it wasn't already reclaimed, and go home to Greystones. As for the water-burst, it was out of their hands so why worry?

As they pondered over their cup of tea Eddie turned to Sean and said, 'I was detained in a cop-shop once before. Remember the blanket-protests Republican prisoners were on in the early Eighties? Well, some local Sinn Feiners organized a sympathy protest in conjunction with the one in Long Kesh. They had it outside the church in Greystones one Sunday. I was goin' by... didn't know what was goin' on. They handed me a blanket an' I joined in. The next thing we were arrested an' brought off to the barracks. We were up in court. They charged us with bein' members of an illegal organization. I was bloody mortified.'

'I never knew that. Were you sent to gaol?'

'Hell, no. I told the truth. I was after havin' a row with the wife an' she put me out of the house. I was down in the dumps. I only joined them for a bit of company an' to keep warm.'

Lar, Sean and Eddie were martyrs to the cause all right – the cause of Wicklow County Council.

Eight hours later they were back in Greystones just in time for the midweek football highlights on BBC.

During the second week of December, London Albion always had a players' Christmas party. Usually it was held at a city hotel, but the previous year it had got totally out of control, so as a precaution it was decided that all future parties would be held in the privacy of the Players' Lounge at Brompton.

Most years they had a fun-theme in relation to the party. For the forthcoming one, it was Ted Brinsley; not that Ted would be present or even aware of the fact. But he was to have a stand-in. Mel Thorpe got in touch with a yogurt producer he knew and borrowed a goat from his farm. The deal was: the goat back first thing in the morning, plus two stand tickets in the event of London Albion getting to a Wembley final.

Mel arrived with the goat, its beard waxed and a clothing of London Albion colours wrapped around its body. Just to allay any uncertainty as to its identity, Mel hung a cardboard sign around its neck with the lettering: Ted Brinsley, Honourable Chairman, London Albion AFC. The goat was given pride of place at the dinner-table.

The players, to a man, were impressed by the goat's impeccable manners. He sat sedately at the top table, placidly surveying the infantile behaviour of the players. It was obvious that he was a pet, a quite gentle character, not deserving of the Ted Brinsley tag left dangling around its neck.

Somewhere during the course of the night, the catering staff grew worried that the goat be unhygienic. Much to the displeasure of the players one of the staff shepherded him outside and put him back in the trailer attached to Mel Thorpe's car. Unfortunately, the tail-gate wasn't properly secured. Within minutes the goat nudged it open and ambled down the road, the Ted Brinsley card still in place around its neck.

The party continued in full swing. When it was over Mel Thorpe drove home. It was only when he saw the flapping tail-gate that he realized the goat was missing. However, as a result of all he had had to drink at the party, he wasn't too worried. The only thing he felt like was a good snooze. Everything would sort itself out in the morning.

And everything did sort itself out in the morning, thanks to the *Daily Mail*. A photo of the goat was emblazoned across the back page, the Ted Brinsley logo showing in bold lettering. The heading read: 'Jekyll and Hyde Albion Chairman'. The accompanying article traced the goat's progress: found wandering around Brompton, about to take up residence inside the gate of a disused church, taken into care at the Dogs and Cats Home. At least Mel Thorpe would know where to go looking.

Ted Brinsley wasn't too happy about the goat and the article in the *Daily Mail*. But he couldn't see any connection between it and London Albion. Not until, that is, he went into Brompton at ten-thirty that morning.

He was walking down the corridor towards the boardroom with one of the office staff.

'What's that?' he said, pointing to the floor.

'Looks like goat droppings.'

'Goat droppings?'

'Yes.'

'Didn't the players have their Christmas party here last night?'

'Yes.'

Straightway Ted Brinsley lost his composure. He blew his top.

Christmas comes but once a year.

Thank God.

9

Gavin and Hammer were allowed home for a week at Christmas. As luck would have it Elaine was also home. Unfortunately, there was to be no Christmas break for Jake. He was too busy doing a whirlwind tour of the Home Counties night-club scene. But he took advantage of Gavin and Hammer's brief exodus to load them down with bulky knick-knacks for Luke's pigeon lofts.

'I though you said the presents were small?'

'They looked small in the shop. It's probably the packaging. Repack them.'

Jake was forever the perpetual nuisance.

Still Luke was thankful for the presents. He didn't get to see much of the lads while they were home as he was working in Mullingar right up until Christmas Eve. And he was due back three days later to help to get the factory ready for stocktaking. The job was still getting him down, but he did his best not to let it show in front of Gavin and Hammer. To add to his problems, his father had a mishap with one of his best pigeons. A few days earlier the weather had been stormy. After Luke's father had finished feeding the pigeons he left a wooden feeding-tray on its side, propped up against a partition. When he went into the loft the next day he found the feeding-tray toppled over – and under it one of his best pigeons, lying limp, its neck broken. It was a previous big-race winner from both Barley Cove and Penzance.

The incident made Luke realize that being away all week just wasn't working out as far as the pigeons were concerned. Apart from the mishap with the feeding-tray most of them were losing condition rapidly. Some had gone into a soft moult, a pathetic sight; the breeding season was going to be a total calamity. Luke could see that his three-day holiday would be taken up by getting his lofts and birds back into shape.

Gavin and Hammer saw a little more of Elaine than they did of Luke. She was home for ten days and wasn't due back to Turin until after New Year's Day. She was on the verge of being off her crutches and was now able to walk quite a bit without their support. They traded football talk and went into Bray with her once or twice.

Gavin and Hammer felt everything would be all right for Elaine. Her injury seemed to be progressing nicely, and her attitude was positive and totally undaunted.

'Have you been talking much to Luke?' she asked.

'Just a little.'

'Did he say anything about his job?'

'No.'

'I don't think he's too happy in it. Do you not think he's gone a bit distant?'

'Luke was always distant,' laughed Gavin. 'There'd be something wrong if he wasn't.'

'That's just it. I think there *is* something wrong.'

'Elaine, you worry too much. Luke is Luke, just leave him be.'

Whatever about Elaine, Gavin and Hammer thought no more of it at the time. After all, as Gavin said, Luke was Luke, and that was the long and short of it. Case closed.

On Christmas morning they met Elaine and went for a short walk down by the Railway Field and out along the Cliff Walk. Christmas morning always had a peacefulness about it – but the Cliff Walk was permanently peaceful. The morning was bright, although frosty. They walked some distance along the Walk, reminiscing about when they used to train along its spectacularly scenic track. Apart from the ordeal of training they had had quite a few laughs on the Cliff Walk when they were kids.

When they came back from their stroll Hammer went over to Elaine's house; he wanted to see her Dad, an ex-professional footballer with Coventry City. He wanted some advice.

'I'm thinkin' of packin' in London Albion at the end of the season and comin' home.'

'Why?'

'Most of the lads we were apprenticed with were let go. Maybe the same's goin' to happen to me. I think they mightn't hold on to me, Anyway some of the U-21s we play with for Ireland play League of Ireland. They say the money's not bad, once you get a job to go along with it. I might give the League of Ireland a try, that's if I could get fixed up with a job.'

'Don't be silly. You're on a full professional contract as it is. Next year, even if your contract is not renewed you're still worth money to the club. At worst, if the club wanted to let you go it would be to another English League club. Either way you can't really lose out.'

'What do you mean, Mr Clarke?'

'Well, if you don't make it with London Albion there's still a future for you with a lower division club. Anyway, who's to say you won't make it with London Albion? Stick it out.'

'Sometimes it isn't easy, Mr Clarke.'

'I know all about it. But it is usually the ones who are capable of sticking it out that have the best chance of making it. Don't be foolish. Now that you've got this far, keep at it. You're not a quitter, are you?'

'I guess not, Mr Clarke.'

'Course you're not. You don't see Elaine wanting to quit, even with all the problems she's having, do you?'

'No. Do you think her knee will be okay?'

'I think that's in the lap of the gods. But she won't fail for lack of trying, the same as you. Another year you'll be over all this self-doubt. It happens to everyone.'

'It hasn't happened to Gavin.'

'Maybe it hasn't, but it's tough for him. People have very high expectations of him. He has to perform week in, week out, to a very high level. That's very tough.'

A few days later, Gavin and Hammer went back to London Albion. Gavin's league debut was only weeks away. Before he left for London he told his family to be available for the big day. He expected them to be there to witness the occasion.

There was talk of a friendly match between Riverside's U-14s and Shamrock Boys during the Christmas break, but Lar Holmes flatly rejected Mr Glynn's overture.

He maintained, 'They'd only break the players up. That's all Riverside want a game for. They'd try and crock a few players and cost us the League.'

Lar had his heart set on winning the Dublin Schoolboys League. The team was odds-on to win the 'D' section. Riverside in a friendly could jeopardize their chances. In Lar's eyes Riverside were like a bunch of Jack Russells any time they came up against his team. No, a friendly against Riverside just wasn't on.

He thought of an excuse so as to put Riverside off the idea of a friendly.

'You have to have the League's permission to play a friendly.'

'No you don't.'

'It's a rule of the Dublin Schoolboys League. All friendlies have to be sanctioned by the League.'

'Since when did you care about rules?'

'What's that supposed to imply?'

'You weren't thinking about rules when you slipped that banger Daisy Dunne on against us two years ago.'

'What d'you mean?'

'You know damn well what I mean.'

'Go to Hell!'

'The same to you.'

End of dialogue between Lar Holmes and Mr Glynn for a good few months, Although on occasion they met at Dublin Schoolboys meetings and sometimes, at a distance, when Lar was motoring around Bray in the County Council truck. It wasn't a sacrificial kind of silence. It didn't cause either man any great discomfort.

Regardless of feuding, or Dublin Schoolboys rules, Riverside got their friendly anyway. It was against Wayside Celtic at the Golden Ball, Kilternan. The team travelled from Bray by minibus. Being Christmas, Mr Glynn got lagged by his wife to visit relatives, so Harry Hennessy had total control.

Harry was itching to ref. He had brought his referee's outfit with him. On the way to Kilternan, Bonkers O'Toole, one of the players, advised him not to get over-involved, that reffing would be too strenuous for him, especially after all the Christmas festivities. But Harry would have none of it. He wanted to ref, all eighteen stone of him, regardless of the consequences.

After fifteen minutes the consequences came home to roost. Harry collapsed in a heap. Two Wayside officials rushed on to the pitch to render medical assistance.

The Riverside kids were quick to gather around him.

Harry was out cold. He looked dead.

'He's a gonner.'

'No, he's not.'

'He's stone-dead. It's all that fat.'

'He's not dead. Look! his belly's movin''

The biggest part of Harry was his belly and, sure enough, it was slowly heaving up and down beneath the black of his referee's outfit. The belly moved again and then his eyes opened.

'Are you all right?' asked one of the men.

' Course he's all right,' roared Bonkers O'Toole. 'He's just havin' a rest. Harry, get up outa that an' don't be makin' a show of yourself.'

Slowly Harry Hennessy came to. They got him back on his feet and assisted him to the sideline. One of the men draped a coat over his shoulders.

'I think you should go to hospital.'

'No, I just slipped and fell over, that's all.'

'You sure?'

'Certain. I'm just a bit shook with the fall. There's a pub across the road, isn't there?'

'Why?'

'A shot of whiskey an' I'll be all right.'

The men weren't at all certain. They thought Harry should go to hospital and get checked out. The Riverside players were of the same opinion. But Harry would have none of it. He walked unassisted to the pavilion to change back into his clothes. One of the Wayside officials could carry on refereeing the match. As far as Harry was concerned he was off to the pub across the road to get himself back into shape. Doctors? Who needed a doctor when there was a pub across the road?

The match recommenced without Harry Hennessy. He had taken up residence in the pub. It ended in a two-all-draw. There was no sign of Harry. He was otherwise engaged.

The Riverside players went looking for Harry. The pub management wouldn't let them in. They spent two hours in the minibus waiting for him to come out. Only that the driver was intent on being paid it would have left without him. Finally, Harry came out and they journeyed back to Bray.

Harry got out last, directly outside his front door. The minibus driver was in for something of a shock. All Harry had left of the thirty pounds minibus fare was a pocket full of loose change and a ten-pound note. He had drunk the rest.

'Happy New Year,' he mumbled to the driver.

'Where's the rest of the fare?'

'The kids'll give it to you.'

'I let them all out down the road.'

'George Glynn'll give it to you.'

'Any chance of you givin' it to me?'

'No. Money's all gone now. See George.'

Harry Hennessy said no more. He gripped his shoddy black football bag, tripped over the edge of the footpath, picked himself up and went into his house. When he got inside he looked out through the curtain to see if the minibus was gone.

It was.

Mr Glynn could pay the balance of the fare. Harry would make up the difference to him sometime. In the long term the matter would blow over. It always did. In the meantime, he stretched out on the sitting-room settee and fell asleep.

He had a dream. He dreamt he was a lad again playing football. Slim, sleek and fast, that was him as a lad.

He was short on memory. A pity he couldn't have video-taped the dream.

Business was brisk for Jake and Tin Knights over Christmas. The only break he got was a few hours on New Year's Day. He went to the cinema with his current girl-friend, a stunning long-haired blonde. Sometime during the show he went out to the foyer to get some popcorn and Coke. When he came back he had trouble finding his seat in the dark interior. He handed his girl-friend a Coke and put his free arm around her. She wasn't very receptive. Next thing, he caught a punch full-square on the jaw. The long-haired blonde he had sat beside was a fellow. Jake collected a few more thumps before he was able to offer an explanation.

The usherette came quickly on the scene. Luckily, his girl-friend was in the row behind and supported his explanation convincingly. At least he didn't get thrown out of the cinema. His jaw hurt like hell, his dignity even more so. He felt uneasy. He and his girl-friend moved to a different part of the cinema.

The name of the film?

It was an oldie: Stephen Spielberg's *Close Encounters of the Third Kind*.

Towards January there was a big freeze-up. The English League and Premiership were virtually closed for two weeks. The long-range weather forecast predicted another week of snow and ice. Ted Brinsley got on the phone in an attempt to organize a game or two outside the country for the first team.

He came up with a jewel. John Warner wasn't too happy.

'Los Angeles, that's a bit much.'

'Two games. You'll be in and out in less than a week.'

'What about jet-lag? The players will be all over the place.'

'This freeze-up will last at least another nine days. Your next Premiership game isn't until the following Saturday. Anyway there's a big match fee in this for the club. Between the fee and the fact that our main sponsors want us out there and, what with the weather, we'd be foolish to refuse.'

'Maybe so.'

'Don't worry, it'll be a cinch.'

Two days later the first team flew out from Heathrow for Los Angeles. They were to play both matches in the Olympic Stadium. One game was to be against the American national team, the other against a club side from Peru.

As they were passing through the main concourse at Heathrow, Dwight Crawford noticed a sports headline in a newspaper in the airport shop.. It read: 'Crawford for England'.

The 'informer' liked that. 'See that, boss, see that.' He rushed into the shop and bought half-a-dozen copies. That heading really went to his head.

All the way from Heathrow to Los Angeles he never shut up about playing for England, and he didn't half get on the other players' nerves.

'Imagine that! "Dwight Crawford plays for England"… 'Dwight Crawford scores for England"…'

'Would you ever shut up.'

The tournament went well. There were no injuries and London Albion won both games. The only problem was at an after-match reception. John Warner wasn't overkeen on receptions, or on the players mixing with the general public, especially the young inexperienced players who would not know what they were letting themselves in for; there were too many hawks hanging around the fringes of the game.

A shady Cockney character named Lennie Parkes approached Chris Morgan, the London Albion centre-forward. John Warner had signed Chris two season previously from Manchester City for one-and-a-quarter million pounds. It almost broke Ted Brinsley's heart at the time to come up with the money. But Chris had been a good investment. He was a regular goalscorer and he had improved the team's standing no end.

'What y' doin' this far west?' asked Chris. Most of the first-team squad knew Lennie from attending matches in London, and occasionally meeting him in night-clubs.

Lennie pulled Chris to one side. He had a proposition to make.

'Want to make a few bob on the side?'

'How much?'

'Three grand.'

'Doin' what?'

'Takin' a little somethin' back to England for me.'

'If it's drugs, forget it.'

'Ain't drugs. Jus' somethin' shiny.'

'Like what?'

'Diamonds.'

'How many?'

'No bigger than an egg cup full.'

'When do I get the money?'

'Soon as you make the handover in London.'

'Four grand.'

'What's a grand among friends? Done!'

'When do I get the diamonds?'

'Tomorrow. Jus' before you get on the plane. See you tomorrow.'

'See you.'

There had been rumours circulating on the night-club scene in London that Lennie Parkes was in the habit of smuggling uncut diamonds into England from the South American diamond-fields. All of a sudden Chris Morgan knew the rumours weren't rumours. They were the truth. Come tomorrow he would be four thousand pounds richer. He knew, of course, that if John Warner got word of what was going on he would be furious., But he need never know.

Unfortunately, John Warner *did* find out. Chris Morgan tangled with Customs officials on the team's arrival back at Heathrow from America. Small as the cache of diamonds was, it was discovered, and Chris was detained. There was quite a furore. A solicitor was sent for. He interviewed Chris in a detention room, but there wasn't a lot he could do. Chris wouldn't be going home. Instead he would be facing a judge. More than likely a two-year jail sentence. John Warner would be on the lookout for a new centre-forward. At least he wouldn't have to go knocking on Ted Brinsley's door looking for another million-and a-quarter pounds.

There was an obvious replacement.

Gavin.

10

Gavin's mother and father, younger brother Garry and sister Debbie flew over from Ireland to witness his first-team debut against Nottingham Forest. They flew into London the night before the game. Gavin and Hammer spent the best part of Friday spring-cleaning the house. Gavin's father was a stickler for cleanliness, especially when someone else was doing the house work. Back home, Hammer had dubbed him 'Mr Sheen'.

'You shouldn't have bothered askin' him over.'

'I had to. He's me Da.'

'Bet he'll go on about how hard a time he had when he worked on the buildings over here. He won't shut up about that.'

Hammer was right. When Gavin's father saw the house, he went into overdrive.

'What's this, Buckingham Palace? The Queen wouldn't have a place like this. Musta cost a fortune. Four bedrooms! What's a fella like you want with four bedrooms?'

Hammer felt like telling the old man that Gavin was thinking of starting a harem, but he restrained himself. Mr Byrne would have blown his top. He was like that once he got going. There was only one thing to do – and that was to switch off.

'I never had nothin' like this. When I came to England four of us had to share a single room. There was only a single room with a wash-hand basin in the corner. We had it rough in those days. The only thing we ever got in England was mullickin' and hardship. Still we managed. All this'll make ye soft.'

'Yes, Da.'

The rest of the family didn't see Gavin's new-found wealth in that light.

'Can we stay over for a week, Da?' asked Garry.

'Like hell! The sooner we get outa this pagan country the better. Soon as the match is over we're off.'

Gavin brought the family out for a meal and his father wasn't long in changing his tune.

'Maybe we'll stay over for a few days. A few days' holiday wouldn't be a bad idea. You wouldn't mind?'

'No, Da. You and Ma could do with a holiday. Stay as long as you like.'

'We never had a holiday before.'

'You can say that again,' added his mother.

'No, we never had a holiday.'

'A holiday? Jimmy, we never even had a honeymoon.'

Having his Ma and Da come over to London meant everything to Gavin. It was great to have his family around him, great to be able to show them around, let them see how well he was doing. It was a pity they wouldn't stay with him all the time. What was a house if there weren't people to give it character, warmth, an atmosphere of being lived in? In short, a home. Maybe they'd come over more often now that they had seen the place.

Maybe.

Gavin's mother was up early the next morning. By the time he came down, she had set the table, cooked some porridge, and had his club blazar, shirt and tie laid out ready for his one-o'clock departure for Brompton.

'Have you got a girl-friend, Gavin?'

'Not really, Ma. There's a few, but nothin' steady.'

'A steady girl-friend would be nice. You should have a steady girl-friend.'

'I'll think about it.'

'You should. Then you'd have someone you could rely on. Has Jake been around to see you since he came over to London?'

'A few times. The record company has him all tied up giggin' and experimentin' with songs. He says he'll be at the match. How's Luke gettin' on?'

'We don't see him. No one sees him. He's supposed to have a job somewhere in the country... Look, I brought you this.'

'What?'

'*The Wicklow People*. It's a special article on you.'

'Let's see.'

Gavin's mother handed him the newspaper. There was a full-page spread – picture and all. Gavin was delighted.

'They've all about me playin' schoolboy – everythin'. Where did they get it all from?'

'Mostly Lar Holmes.'

'Ma, it's great. Thanks.'

'Everybody's keeping their fingers crossed, Gavin. They want you to do well this afternoon.'

'Ma, I hope I don't let them down.'

'You won't, Gavin. Just remember we're all with you. Sink or swim, everything will just be the same. And another thing...'

'What, Ma?'

'That's why you'd be better off with a steady girl-friend. She'd be there to stand by you. It's all very fine to have lots of friends, but when all's said and done there's not many you can really count on. Understand?'

'Yes, Ma.'

'There's one other thing.'

'What?'

'Good luck this afternoon.'

Hammer came downstairs. He went to a cupboard and got out some cornflakes.

'You could do with something better than that,' interjected Mrs Byrne. 'Let me get you a proper breakfast.'

'He was out late. He wouldn't be able for a lot.'

'Still, he could do better than cornflakes. Have you no match today, Shane?'

'I wouldn't have been out late if I had. I'll be goin' with you to watch Gavin play.'

'Now that Gavin's on the first team you'll have to move up with him.'

'Not if Scotch Pete has his say.'

'Who's Scotch Pete?'

'The fella Hammer'll have to get off the team if he wants to get his place.'

'Well, you can start that now, by taking porridge instead of cornflakes for your breakfast. You don't mind porridge, do you?'

'No, Mrs Byrne. Not if you give me toast and marmalade with it.'

Gavin was only too delighted to have his family around him on the morning of his team debut. There would have been nothing as bad as moping around an empty house waiting for the hours to pass until kick-off time. Making his debut at Brompton would be tough; if the game had been away from home there would have been less pressure on him. It wasn't as if he was an unknown stepping on to the public stage for the first time. There had been snatches of hype in the newspapers, lots of exposure in London Albion's fanzine about his exploits on the reserves. His fans expected a lot. Even those club supporters who hadn't seen much of him in action knew what to expect. If he didn't play up to form they'd be very disappointed. First impressions were always important. If he had a bad game it wouldn't be long before the 'boo' boys would be out in force. No, he was glad his Ma and Da had come over to give some moral support.

At one o'clock Gavin had to leave for the half-hour drive from house to ground. Sometimes the team had a pre-match lunch at a nearby hotel. But a pre-match lunch was out for the Forest game. His family would follow on with Hammer, nearer to kick-off time.

Gavin arrived at Brompton half-an-hour early. He had got the time wrong! One of the office staff called him over.

There was a telex from Elaine in Italy wishing him well on his debut. Elaine was having it tough.

Maybe he should ring her after the match, let her know how he got on.

There was a second message. Jake and Dave would be at the match. Jake had spent half the previous night trying to ring Gavin, but each time the line was engaged. No wonder! Gavin's sister had spent the evening phoning her friends back home in Greystones.

Gavin took a peek out on to the pitch. All the early arrivals were in place. Mostly kids, running in and out between the rows of seats. He went down to the dressing-rooms. Syd Davison was hanging the first-team kit in place.

'You're early?'

'I got the times mixed up.'

'Nervous?'

'A bit.'

'It's the right way to feel. Keeps ye on yer toes. Debut matches ye never forget. Stevie Hodgson tol' me to wish ye well.'

'Will he be at the match?'

'No, he's up in Halifax, watchin' some player a scout wants him to sign for the Youths.'

'Pity.'

'Bill Thornbull'll be here, though. I want to tell ye something after the match.'

'Tell me now.'

'No. Ye have to prove yerself first. I'll tell ye after the match.'

Syd threw Gavin a match programme and went searching in a cupboard beside the shower-room door. The match ball had to be got ready – and tie-ups were very important. Not forgetting Doublemint for the chewers. And the towels, for the after-match showers. Professional footballers – like babies – had to have everything done for them.

Gavin got stuck into the programme. To his delight there was an article on him.

'Don't let that go to yer head. It's only print. Print don't put the ball into the back of the net.'

Gavin just grinned. Next thing, the players were arriving. They shoved and jostled one another, and generally messed about until John Warner put in an appearance. That shut them up.

John Warner always gave a full team talk before the players togged out. Then he'd leave the dressing-room, returning later just before they were due to go out on the pitch. He would go to each player individually, gee them up and send them out all fired-up to deprive the opposition of victory.

'You can't win all the time. That's not the end of the world. But if you lost this one, that is the end of the world.'

John Warner didn't like to lose. He expected his players to be like-minded.

For Gavin, the pep-talk and togging out seemed a blur, probably because he was so tensed up. Next thing, the referee came to check their football studs and make sure any rings the players wore were either taken off of taped over. He gave a quick run down on how he expected them to behave, and the repercussions to be expected if they got out of line. Most of the players did some light warm-up exercises as he gave his summary of the rules and the spirit in which the game should be played. Then it was out into the corridor to line up beside Nottingham Forest and wait for the official nod to make the walk along the corridor and out on to the pitch.

It wasn't long in coming. Brompton was jammed. The clamour didn't abate for a full two minutes.

'Albion!' 'Albion!'

'Forest!' 'Forest!'

And so it went on, a huge explosion of chants around the stadium. Albion kicked about at the Clock-End, the end where the most die-hard of Albion supporters congregated. The Clock's famous round shape showed the time to be five-to-three. Gavin warmed up with a few shots on the goalkeeper plus three or four short sprints along the width of the penalty area. The flat back-four John Warner intended to play kept close to the centre-circle in a diamond formation, knocking a few balls to one another. Scotch Pete, the main pivot of the defence, stood nonchalantly knocking balls about. For him, it was as if the deafening chants of the crowd didn't exist. He was oblivious to it all, except when the crowd began to chant his name. Then he raised a hand in acknowledgement and got on with spraying the ball about among his fellow defenders.

Privately, John Warner was expecting a lot from Gavin. He expected the midfield of Mick Bates, Mel Thorpe Dwight Crawford and Craig Shortall to set up a lot of chances for Gavin and Bobby Turner, his attacking partner up front. Nottingham Forest were good in midfield. But John Warner was really pleased with his own midfield lately. He was sure they would dominate Forest. They were very quick to the ball and creative. They'd be certain to put Forest under the cosh, thus creating plenty of opportunities for Gavin and Bobby Turner.

Mel Thorpe, the London Albion captain, went to the centre-circle for the toss. Meanwhile Syd Davison came on to the pitch and gathered the tracksuit tops from the London Albion players. Forest won the toss. They elected to play into the Clock-End for the first half.

'Forest Choppers!'

'Los Angeles!' (a reference to the unfortunate Chris Morgan).

The game was on. Almost immediately the London Albion midfield put the clamps on. They stifled Forest. Gave them no room to move in. They had the Forest engine-room under control. Forest couldn't even kick-start; Mick Bates and Mel Thorpe were on to them too

113

quickly. Dwight Crawford was greased-lightning coming forward on the right. But he wasn't of that much benefit to Gavin; he kept going on his own. He shaved the left-hand upright twice, and almost knocked the goalkeeper cold with a thunderbolt of a shot. Twice he should have squared the ball to Gavin. Gavin cursed his luck. Dwight was out to impress, conscious that the England manager was sitting snugly in the directors' box passing a knowledgeable eye over proceedings.

He had even added an extra touch of Brylcreem to his hair before coming out. It was 'now or never' for him. Once he got sight of goal he had no intention of parting with the ball. He was out to prove that he was the new Bobby Charlton as far as goal-scoring was concerned.

Come half-time the score was nil-all. John Warner was disappointed though not despondent. He gave Dwight Crawford hell.

'What do you think you're doing?'

'What y' mean, boss?'

'You won't spread the ball. Every chance you get you're straight for goal. You're not bringing other players into the game, even if they're in a better scoring position. Keep that up and you won't be long coming off.'

'Boss, the England manager's out there. I have to impress him. I wanna play for England.'

'You want to play for England? Keep that up and you won't be playing for anyone, much less England. Pure selfishness. Football's a team game. You play for the team. Got me?'

'Sure, boss. But what about England?'

'Hump them. They don't pay your wages, do they?'

'No, boss.'

'Get out there and do your bit. Spread the ball about and do your bit for the team or you'll find yourself going home on a bicycle.'

'What does that mean, boss?'

'You'll get the sack.'

Dwight Crawford played a lot better in the second half. That is he played for the team, not for himself. As a consequence, Gavin flourished. He got a lot more quality ball, and he certainly showed most of his potential. The fans were taking note.

'I heard of that kid. Didn't think he was that good.'

'That good? He's only half playin'. I saw him for the Youths. He's magic. Wait until he gets the ball around the box.'

The fans didn't have too long to wait. About fifteen minutes into the second half, Mel Thorpe played a ball wide to Craig Shortall. Craig carried the ball forward and played a one-two with Gavin on the edge of the Forest area. Craig slipped the ball past the goalkeeper, only to see it come off the bottom of the upright. Gavin was in like a shot and slid the ball into the back of the net. He turned, gestured skywards. The crowd was in raptures; the stadium was a sea of green and white.

The ball was recentred, and the crowd sat back in anticipation of a flood of goals to come.

Dwight Crawford put on a dazzling performance, spreading the ball about and getting in some telling runs at the Forest defence. Mel Thorpe was hard but fair; Mick Bates something similar. Scotch Pete was, as expected, a rock in defence. Craig Shortall was a little off key, but that didn't really matter; the midfield was functioning well enough anyway. The two fulls were sound and gave that extra width coming from the back. The 'keeper was safe. Gavin and Bobby Turner up front were hitting it off well together. It was obvious they would make a good partnership. But as well as London Albion played the second goal never came. As things turned out Gavin's goal was the match-winner. London Albion won one–nil.

Back in the dressing-room Syd Davison came straight over to Gavin. 'Remember I told ye there was somethin' I wanted to tell ye after the match... Well, all the great goalscorers score on their debuts. Y've done that. Y're goin' to be one of the great ones.'

Gavin felt chuffed. One of the great ones? He felt his performance didn't deserve such a high accolade. One of the great ones? Maybe so, maybe not. Later, in the Players' Lounge, Gavin introduced John Warner to his family.

'You must have been a pretty good player in your day,' said John to Mr Byrne.

'Not bad. Though Gavin takes it from the wife's side of the family. Her father and brothers were good footballers. The only thing I was ever good at was winnin' the toss.'

'And fixin' things around the house, Da.'

'I hope you haven't got a job in mind.'

'There's a tap needs fixin' back at the house,' laughed Gavin. 'You can fix it before you go home.'

'Thanks very much... Gavin has it in the feet. With me it's in the hands. Only thing, I don't get paid a patch of what you're givin' him. That's the way the world's gone. Crazy! He's not a bad lad, though. He sees us all right.'

'Don't forget the tap, Da.'

Gavin's father didn't forget the tap. He fixed it first thing Sunday morning. Then he read the reports on the match against Nottingham Forest in the Sunday papers. Gavin got a favourable mention.

Gavin's father scratched his head.

Some sons had all the luck.

Apart from football, Mr Glynn's Toyota was his pride and joy. He and Harry Hennesy were in the habit of scouting around Bray in it, doing a tour of the housing-estates, on the watch-out for an unknown star that might strengthen Riverside's U-14s. The team was doing very well lately. Another class addition to the squad and they could very well be shoving for promotion to the 'A' section before the season was out.

Mr Glynn had a great eye for a player – Harry was merely his back-up man, a second opinion so to speak.

Over the years he had picked up a lot of useful players, watching kids kick ball on the local housing estates. Some of his best players had been spotted in kick-abouts. He was never long in following up a lead either. If anyone passed on word about a good player he would get into his car straightway and check out the information. He could charm kids without any trouble. Once he found a likely prospect he'd have him signed on the dotted line in next to no time.

Mr Glynn wasn't too bothered where he got his players. Sometimes he poached them from other clubs.

Shankill was a favourite poaching ground. Every time the local schoolboy soccer hierarchy saw Mr Glynn's car in the vicinity they knew he was on the trail of a Shankill player.

'Glynn's on the prowl again.'

'I wonder who he's after this time?'

'Does it matter? He has some neck, that lad. You'd think he'd cop on an' not be poachin' kids from other clubs. I'm sick of him comin' to me door with a transfer form in one hand an' a handshake with the other.'

'By the look of things you're goin' to see him again soon. He's been around lately. Kids say he's watchin' Jim Lynch.'

'Jim Lynch's our best U-14.'

'Was. Glynn's after him.'

Mr Glynn wasn't long in making an appearance.

'What d'you want?'

'I want you to sign a transfer form.'

'For who?'

'Jim Lynch.'

'I'm not signin' any form. Jim Lynch's our best player. Any decent player I ever had you took. I'm not signing no form. Go to Hell.

'You can't refuse a transfer.'

'I can.'

'You won't sign the transfer?'

'No. Get somebody else to sign it.'

Mr Glynn found the door closed in his face. He folded the transfer form, put it back into his pocket and drove off in the Toyota to locate Shankill's second-in-command. As far as he was concerned he wasn't poaching anybody. Jim Lynch wanted the transfer. He wanted to sign for Riverside Boys. If the player wanted to move that was the player's entitlement. In Mr Glynn's eyes he hadn't attempted to poach Jim Lynch. On the contrary, Jim Lynch had approached *him*. Well, in a roundabout way. Poaching players... it was a very grey area. Mr Glynn worked well in grey areas. He was a master of rules and regulations. He could work them every time.

He got his transfer form signed. Jim Lynch was now officially a Riverside player. Very soon afterwards, Riverside would be shoving hard for the runners-up spot in the 'B' section.

Football matches weren't just won on the field, they were won off it. Riverside were on song. They would take some beating.

Lar Holmes and Shamrock Boys U-14s were still top of the 'D' section of the Dublin Schoolboys League. Everything was going according to plan. It was odds-on they were going to win the League. The other top teams were all taking points off one another. As for Shamrock Boys they were unbeaten, with a much easier end-of-season run-in than the other teams in contention. What was more, Gavin's brother Garry was banging the goals in week after week. He was a regular goal scorer, a certainty to turn a match on its head.

Lar had two worries: One was the 'Woodbine Duo'. They had become very cheeky lately and he was having problems disciplining them. But they loved football too much to risk being suspended. Most of their cheek was confined to the minibus coming home from matches. Lar could bear that, even though he was the recipient of most of it. He'd hold his peace; winning the League title was more important than reprimanding the Woodbine Duo and risk having them walk out on the team.

The other problem wouldn't surface until the end-of - season evening matches. Lar had two ex-Gaelic players on his panel. He was worried that come the end of season they'd go missing to play Gaelic. He'd have to watch that one. Be real nice to both of them. Not upset them and have them sulking off to Eire Óg.

For the moment, however, Lar felt snug, managing the team that was walking away with the 'D' section of the Dublin Schoolboys League. Even Riverside in Bray were full certain Shamrock Boys would win the 'D' section. Lately, when driving around Bray in the County Council truck, some of the Riverside players were shouting 'Once-off' at him. Lar had never won a League title of any description before. This was to be his first time.

'Hey, Once-off! You'll never win a League title again. It'll be your first an' your last.'

First and last? It would only be the beginning.

'Hey, Once-off, remember us?'

Lar just grinned.

'Remember the Alamo.'

The Alamo? Riverside were Apaches. What had the Apaches got to do with the Alamo?

Nothing.

Remember the Alamo.

Forget it.

Jake, Dave and Tin Knights were billed for a glamour Saturday night gig at London's Marqee. Gavin and Hammer were in attendance. Tin Knights were well received and they made an impression.

During a break in the session Jake and Dave went over to the bar and had a drink with Gavin and Hammer. As they sat there laughing and joking, an onlooker with one too many under the belt came over to Jake and started making a nuisance of himself. Jake told him to clear off.

'Irish pig.'

A few more taunts followed.

Jake bore up well, but not Hammer. He turned from the bar, and without a second's warning floored the drunk with a right upper-cut. Straightway the club's bouncers were on the spot. They grabbed Gavin and Hammer and shoved them towards a side door.

'There's a taxi-rank across the road,' muttered one of the bouncers in a heavy Cork accent. 'Get over to it and get out of here as quick as you can. Your man's got mates. They'll come lookin' for you.'

Gavin and Hammer didn't have to be told a second time. They went straight over to the taxi-rank and were well away before anyone came looking for them.

Jake and Dave had to go back on stage and finish off the gig, but luckily there was no further trouble. The drunk and his mates were in a kind of forgiving mood. But only for the quick thinking of the bouncers things could have turned out a lot differently. Sometimes it wasn't fun being Irish in England. There was always a certain element lurking in the background spoiling for a fight.

Luckily London Albion didn't get to hear about Hammer clouting the drunk. John Warner would have been furious. But it served as a warning to be wary of the public, especially in night-clubs.

Jake and Dave didn't come out of it to well though. They got a rollicking from both the record company and their management. It was a black mark against them.

'Any more trouble and…'

'And?'

'Your contracts could be terminated.'

Midweek, the week after, Gavin and Hammer were over in Ireland for a European Championship U-21 fixture against Switzerland. Both teams were out of the running.

Scotland, the top team in the group, had already qualified. The game was due to be played under lights at the Showgrounds in Sligo.

The players felt a little put out with the idea of playing in Sligo. It meant having to travel the breadth of the country by coach, not that the journey in itself was any great ordeal, but some of the players had already made long coach trips the previous day to get connecting flights to Ireland. However, none of them complained; it went hand in hand with being selected. Anyway, the FAI wanted to bring representative soccer to the provinces. It was their way of promoting the game.

Things were on the up-and-up for Gavin. In the preceding month and a half he had become a regular on London Albion's first team and the Press had latched on to him – the Irish papers in particular. They were touting his name for a possible call-up to the senior Republic of Ireland squad. But for the rest of the lads on the U-21 squad who were with big-name clubs the future wasn't looking quite so rosy. Some of them were becoming disenchanted with soccer, losing heart, thinking of throwing in the towel as far as making it at the top grade. Their enthusiasm and dedication was beginning to slip. Five years of hard slogging and the dream was beginning to turn more than a little sour. It was a dangerous and destructive period in their football lives. The gloss was being taken away, the sparkle removed; their zeal for the sport wasn't the same, expectations were beginning to lower. They would have been less than human if they hadn't felt envious of Gavin: a Premier Division player, a certainty to play for the full Irish international team some day. Not only that, he had an agent – one of the best.

An agent? It had happened about two weeks earlier. A knock came on the door. It was an agent who wanted to sign him, wanted to represent him. Gavin asked some of the first-team players for advice, what should he do. They said, 'Sign, he's one of the best going, honest.'

121

Gavin signed up. His old contract with London Albion would be up for renewal in August. The agent promised him a more lucrative one. John Warner and Sam Gregson weren't too happy with the news. Ted Brinsley was even less happy, but he had to put up with the fact. A lot of side-money would be going into other pockets, money that could be going into his own pocket, Agents! Ted had no time for them. Gavin would be well looked after. Too well looked after – in Ted's eyes.

On and off the pitch, the match against Switzerland was a huge success. The whole of the North-West soccer fraternity must have been present. The Showgrounds was jammed and the attendance got value for money, even though the Republic was held to a one-all draw. Gavin put in a top-rate performance although he didn't score. It was easy to see why he was beginning to cause such a stir across channel and to understand why lately he had become a permanent fixture on London Albion's Premiership team.

He was in a class of his own. It was obvious he was capable of making the transition to full international football. After the game a member of the FAI hierarchy more or less told him so.

'You could very well make the next European Championship panel.'

'Think so?'

'Sure. It's fixed for June, away to Austria. Don't be surprised if we're in touch.'

The full international panel! The European Championships! Gavin hardly believed it could happen so quickly. Sligo wasn't such a wasted trip after all.

While Gavin was thriving on the packed-stadium atmosphere of first-team games, Hammer was playing his schedule of reserve-team matches on sometimes lifeless training grounds. There was hardly a word of encouragement, a show of appreciation. Never a mention in the

Press. He had to generate his own motivation, his own sense of progression. The opposition was always mean, stayed mean, and the meanest of all were the empty stadia. In a way it steeled his character. He had hardened, developing an immunity to all the empty depression around him, the dull leaden skies, the duller emptiness of the absence of spectators.

When they played at home he began to recognize each supporter, where they sat or stood, and every remark they would pass, and exactly when they would cheer or boo. He wondered if they knew in advance what moves he would make, how he would react to a situation, how he would repulse an attack. Sometimes he felt like shouting on to the terraces and asking them their names, but somehow that would have broken the whole hypnotic drabness of reserve-team football, and perhaps he would have woken up as if from a dream and found himself outside Luke's loft in Greystones, waiting for the pigeons to return home.

For Hammer, there was none of the excitement Gavin was feeling. Just the hope that he would be kept on with the reserves, just the hope that they would extend his one-year contract for another season. At least he was not on the injury list. On London Albion's books two or three players always seemed to be fighting their way back after injury. Their injuries would mend for a while, but would recur. A quick cortizone injection would fail to work and they would become permanent crocks, not able to make it back on to the first team, then struggling in the reserves or 'A' team. The only way out for them at the end of the day was an insurance pay-out and a premature ending to their football career.

For Hammer, there were disappointments, but not despair. There were more than straws to be clutched at – that some day he would make the breakthrough, just like Gavin.

11

Unfortunately, Elaine had suffered a setback with her ligament injury. Until recently everything had been progressing according to plan. But in the last few weeks her knee became sore and swollen after jogging. She was reassessed by a specialist and passed on to another one in Brussels, who put her through a revolutionary treatment for serious knee injuries. The only bright spot was that before putting her through the torture of regaining her fitness Juventus decided to let her go back to Ireland for a week's holiday in order to perk up her morale. The stipulations they made was that she would do some light jogging and keep to the diet recommended to all Juventus players during the football season.

Elaine enjoyed her week's visit home. The Ladies FAI heard she was back and invited her to observe one of their squad training-sessions. Elaine declined.

'Wait until I'm fit again. Then if you want me, come and get me.'

It wasn't that she was snubbing them. She just couldn't see any point in attending training-sessions, not until it was obvious that her injury was going to mend satisfactorily. There was another consideration; she had already come to know a lot about ladies' soccer – more than most people connected with the Irish game would ever know. If she were selected to play for Ireland, there was always the possibility that the home association wouldn't be able to afford the insurance cover Juventus would demand. Deep in her heart she knew that as long as she was playing professional football in Italy it would be highly unlikely she would ever play international football. Anyway, the whole issue would have to be put on the back-burner as long as her injury persisted.

Greystones in the middle of March was a very gloomy place, especially if the weather was wet, and there was plenty of rain while Elaine was home.

She remembered Jake once saying, 'Depressed? Talk about people bein' depressed. Even the dogs are depressed in Greystones.' There wasn't much to do. She saw Lar Holmes just once, and that was in the Railway Field one Thursday night in the lashing rain. He had the U-14s lapping the pitch, squelching about on the mud at the side of the pitch. Lar was delighted to see her.

'Goin' to march in the St Patrick's Day parade with us, Elaine?'

'Don't think so, Lar. Not if the weather's like this.'

And the weather was like that. It rained bucketfuls. But she got a glimpse of the Parade. Lar had organized a Council truck, thinly disguised with heavy sheets of cardboard and bunting, as a float to carry his U-14 squad on.

But everybody knew it was the Council truck, what with Lar, Sean Dunlop and Eddie Reilly on board. Most of the U-14s didn't bother showing up. They believed the whole idea of appearing in the St Patrick's Day Parade was stupid, so they gave it a miss. But Lar, Sean and Eddie diligently carried the flag for Shamrock Boys. Eddie and Sean even went to the extreme of dressing up as footballers. Eddie had got the boot-polish out and dressed as Pele. Sean was got up as Gazza. He had a pillow shoved underneath the belly of the England football jersey he wore.

Someone shouted, 'Where're you goin', Gazza? To play for England?'

Back came the curt reply, 'No, to Holles Street Hospital to have me baby.'

Lar sat in the cab driving the truck, unaware of the antics behind him.

The glimpse Elaine got of the float passing along

Church Road made her glad she had decided not to join the Parade. Sean and Eddie's antics were making a show of Shamrock Boys. Questions would be asked at the next committee meeting. It wouldn't be the only place. Lar's overseer on the Council would also be asking what an unauthorised Council truck was doing in a St Patrick's Day Parade?

But worse was to follow after the parade. Lar went quietly home while Sean and Eddie went on a pub-crawl in their fancy-dress outfits. They did the Beach House first, then the Burnaby. Finally they went to the La Touche Hotel, where the management refused them entry. Threatening revenge, they went to Lar Holmes's house and asked him to open the cab of the Council truck to look for a lost sweater. They rummaged around, found a stop-cock and marched back to the La Touche Hotel. Outside, on the pavement, they opened up a stop-cock cover and turned off the water supply to the La Touche. Then they marched in triumph back to the Beach House and spent the remainder of St Patrick's Day deep in satisfaction at a task well done. Outside it was raining cats and dogs. The only really dry place in Greystones was the La Touche Hotel.

Elaine never got to know about the La Touche Hotel; that was to remain a private matter between Sean and Eddie and, perhaps, the hotel management. But one thing did strike her. Greystones was no longer part of her life. Gavin, Hammer, Jake and, to a lesser extent, Luke, were all gone. Greystones was a place of the past, their futures lay elsewhere. It was sad in a way to realize that the town that had nurtured them as children couldn't sustain them as adults. They had all had to leave Greystones to make a living. It was a sobering fact, reflected in many small towns and villages throughout Ireland. Maybe being Irish didn't necessarily mean being born in Ireland. She was one of that breed herself, born in England of Irish parents. Maybe for some, being Irish was a sense of spirit rather than location. If ever there was a tribe born to wander it was the Irish. And just being back in Greystones proved that. Look at the lads, most of their school pals, they were all gone.

On the Saturday, the day before Elaine was due to go back to Turin, she was in Bray checking up on some old school-friends from her Loreto days. More by accident than design she came across Luke. He looked a mess, pale and highly irritable. The deterioration was deplorable.

At first he didn't have a lot to say. Elaine got the impression that he wanted to run away and hide, that he didn't really want to talk to her. But after a few minutes he thawed and Elaine got him to go into a coffee shop with her and, hopefully, get what was bothering him off his mind.

'Luke, what's up with you?'

'Nothin'.

'There *is* something. It shows. Are you working?'

'Yeah, down in Mullingar, I get home for the weekends.'

'There's something wrong. Are you not hitting it off at home?'

'At home? Everythin's fine at home. Everythin's fine. There's nothin' wrong.'

'If that's the case it must be in your job. What are you working at, Luke?'

'Elaine, it's none of your business. It's nothin' to do with you.'

'Tell me as a friend.'

'I don't think I should. It's kinda personal.'

'That's why you need to tell someone. Tell me.'

'Maybe there is somethin' wrong. Maybe I'm readin' too much into things. It's not that I don't want a job. Well, I don't really like what I'm workin' at. I want to give it up, but me Da would probably do his nut if I did. It's about the only job I've been able to get since I left school. I don't like it, Elaine, but what can I do?'

'Talk it over with your father. He'd probably understand. You'd get another job sometime.'

'That's where you're wrong, Elaine. I don't think I'd ever get another job.'

'What do you work at anyway?'

'It's a deboning factory. We cut up meat and that kind of thing. It's pretty gruesome. It's getting me down, having to deal with carcasses.'

'For God's sake give up the job. I'll see your father.'

'Don't, Elaine. Please don't. I'll get out of it sometime soon. I'll just have to hang on another while and see if somethin' better comes up. If I tell you somethin', promise you won't tell anyone.'

'I promise. But for God's sake give up the job. It's not worth it. It's damaging your health.'

'There's a slaughter-yard beside the deboning shed. Most days up to twenty cows are slaughtered ... Elaine, I'm goin' to set the place on fire.'

'You're what?'

'I'm goin' to burn the place to the ground. I'm dead against it.'

'You can't do that. They'd lock you up.'

'I don't care. This thing is buggin' me for months. I have to do it. It's slaughter, murder, call it what you like, Elaine, it's goin' to happen. I have it all worked out.'

'Luke, don't go back to that place.'

Luke was beginning to get emotional. He was on the verge of breaking down.

'Luke, promise me you'll do nothing. For God's sake, don't set that place on fire. Give me two weeks. I'll see what I can do. I might be able to help get you another job. Can you give me a phone number where I can contact you?'

'Elaine, don't tell me Da what I told you. Please don't tell him.'

'I won't. Give me two weeks. In the meantime, if you need anyone to talk to here's my phone-number in Turin. Don't be afraid to ring me. Remember, I'm your friend,

Luke. I'm there to help.'

Luke didn't reply straight off. But the words triggered off something inside him. All of a sudden he found himself apologising to Elaine for bothering her.

'Forget it, Luke.'

But Elaine knew that Luke wouldn't forget. There was something deep down that had triggered off his unbalanced state of mind. She'd get in touch with Jake. Of all the lads, Jake was the closest to Luke. Jake should be able to help. What was more, he cared about Luke. He was the person to see. He wouldn't let Luke down.

They parted company outside the cafe; Luke to get the bus back to Greystones, Elaine to meet her friends.

'Don't worry, Elaine. I'll be all right.'

Elaine smiled, shook his hand. But deep down she was worried sick.

Luke walked up the Main Street towards the Greystones bus-stop.

The bus to nowhere. Maybe that was part of the problem.

If only it were. No, he knew it was more complex than that.

He was sick in the head.

That evening Elaine phoned Jake; she got him at the third attempt. She pulled no punches. Told Jake that Luke's mental health was under threat.

'He's threatened to burn down an abattoir.'

'What abattoir?'

'The abattoir beside where he works. Jake, you're the one he gets on best with. He hates his job. He needs to get away. He's going to crack-up if he doesn't get help.'

'Elaine, how the hell can I help? I'm not a psychologist.'

'Bring him over to London, Let him stay with you. Try and get him a job.'

'You're not askin' much, are you? Why don't Gavin and Hammer help?'

'No. You're the one he looks up to. You're the one he'd rather stay with. Jake, you've got to do something. You're his only hope.'

'Right, Elaine, I'll see what I can do. But I still think it's not fair to dump him on me.'

'Not fair? Do you want to see him locked up for burning down a slaughter-house?'

'Give me your phone-number. I'll see the band manager. He might give him a job as a roadie... Elaine, he won't come over here and burn the place down, will he?'

'No, of course not. He just needs to get away and have a job he likes. He needs to be among friends.'

'Easy on, Elaine. Anyway, he mightn't want to come over. He'd have to get rid of his pigeons.'

'He knows what's at stake. He'll go over.'

'Right, Elaine. I'll ring you back next week.'

'No, Thursday night of this week.'

'Thursday night? You're not givin' me much time.'

'Time? He could have the slaughter-house burned down by then.'

First thing the following morning Jake rang Morris Evans, Tin Knights' manager, at his office. Morris wasn't available.

'I don't want to talk to him on the phone. I'd rather have an appointment.'

'Will four-thirty this afternoon do?'

'Sure. Four-thirty. How's business comin' along?'

'Just fine. We've a few extra bookings for you.'

Jake hung up. Hopefully, Morris Evans would be in the right frame of mind when Jake asked for a job for Luke. It would be no great sacrifice for Morris. Apart from Tin Knights he had three top-class groups under his tutelage and business was good. His speciality was concerts, some of which were huge open-air promotions. The company's juggernauts travelled the whole country, up into Scotland and west through Wales. There was a huge back-up of roadies, riggers and technicians to put up the props, stage lighting and sound equipment into place. Luke could drive, he was handy at electrical work and carpentry. He'd fit in and be worth his keep. There should be no difficulty finding him a job. Keep him around until he found his feet, got whatever it was that was bugging him out of his system.

Jake reckoned Luke would be taken on. Morris was pleased with the way Tin Knights were progressing. He wouldn't want to upset Jake and thus rock the boat. If not, Jake would deliver that extra bit of coaxing. If ever Luke had a friend, it was Jake.

Friday night when Luke came home from Mullingar there was a message for him to ring Jake in London. The job offer was made.

'Are you comin' over or not?'

'Don't know.'

'The job's waitin' for you. All you have to do is show up. You'll like workin' around bands.'

'It's a bit sudden. I'd like more time to think it over.'

'I don't know why you need to think it over. It's not like you'd be on your own. You'd be stayin' with me. You'd see Gavin and Hammer now and then.'

'Jake, I couldn't go this Monday, I'd have to sort the pigeons out. See that they were looked after.'

'Your Da could do that.'

'No. I'd have to see that they were left with the right people. Anyway, I don't really want to give up me pigeons.'

'What's more important, your pigeons or a job?'

'Jake, let me think it over. I'll ring you back Sunday night.'

'Elaine was on to me, said things weren't goin' too well for you. You'd be better off over here, Luke. No dead-ends and that.'

'Is that all she said?'

'Yeah, that was about it,' lied Jake. 'She was worried the

job you're in was a dead loss and it was gettin' you down.'

'She said nothin' else?'

'No, that was it. Short and sweet.'

Of course there was more. The bit about burning down the slaughter-house and going off the loop. But he just couldn't come out with it. Luke would go totally haywire. He'd give right up on the idea of going over to London.

'Jake, I'll ring back on Sunday night and let you know for certain.'

'Right, see you.'

'All the best, and thanks.'

Saturday morning Luke went into Bray to see if the Bray Pigeon Club would organize an auction of his birds if he went to work in London. He felt there should be no problem auctioning them off. Quite a few fanciers would be only too willing to pay big money for most of his stock. So far he had said nothing to his parents. They could wait. There was no point in telling them his plans if he couldn't make arrangements for his pigeons. They came first. If they couldn't be properly looked after he just wouldn't go to London.

It was a big decision for Luke though. He didn't really want to give up his pigeons. But there was a chance that by going to London he'd have a good job and he'd be able to pull himself together. The way he was now – everything was slipping away. He could sense he was going downhill rapidly. The nightmares, the impulse to set the slaughter-house on fire, everything. Even to face people, having to talk to them was a chore. No, getting away to London would be a blessing in disguise. He'd have Jake, Gavin and Hammer. The laughs would come back into his life. He'd come out of himself. It would be a new start, a chance to finally sort himself out. And Jake would help. Jake had always been like a brother to him. Jake understood. He could trust Jake.

When in Bray Luke rang Arthur Irvine in Portadown.

Arthur was sorry to hear Luke was getting out of the pigeon-racing scene. Luke offered him a few birds but he declined.

'You could do with the money. Put them in the auction, that way you'll have some money to fall back on if things go wrong in London. What's more – have the auction in Dublin, not Bray. Get the Bray lads to mind your birds until then. They can set up the auction and all for you. Don't worry, things will work out.'

'I don't like handin' over the birds, Arthur. They're everythin' to me. Sure you don't want the King's Cup winner?'

'Well, maybe it. Maybe as a memento.'

'You'll be down for it?'

'I'll be down for the auction. Give it to one of the Bray lads and they can hand it over then.'

'I'll do that, Arthur. And thanks for all you've done for me.'

'No problem, Luke. I hope all goes well for you in London.'

By Saturday evening all the arrangements were in place. A phone call to Dublin and the auction date and venue were arranged. The following Saturday Luke was to get his birds into Bray and the committee of the Bray club would hold them in their lofts until the date arrived. Effectively, his pigeon-racing career was at an end. All that remained was to tell his parents he was going to London to work. They didn't disagree.

He rang Jake. Told him he'd be in London the following Sunday and to meet him at Euston. Monday to Friday he finished off his job in Mullingar. Saturday he got his pigeons in to Bray; the lofts could be dismantled later and sold locally. Saturday night he packed his case. Sunday morning he got the boat from Dun Laoghaire.

On the ship he stood by the rail, watching the coastline fade from view. He could make out the outline of the Sugar Loaf and Bray Head, and all the other dark shapes of mountains brooding on the horizon.

He turned and faced the open sea. The wind ruffled his hair and stung his face to the very bone. He stood motionless. The white flickering of seagulls followed the ship across the Irish Sea. Luke watched them, dreading that images of pigeons would show among the white-bellied gulls.

The wind traced rain. Luke could feel it dampen across his face.

Still he watched the gulls.

The imaginary image of pigeons failed to appear.

Luke felt that everything was going to be all right.

Behind was home.

Ahead, a new future.

Hopefully, his nightmares were at an end.

12

Sometimes a team's bad fortune has a habit of repeating itself. London Albion had progressed to the semi-final of the Coca-Cola Cup only to be knocked out by Arsenal. Still only mid-table in the Premiership, London Albion were putting together a good run in the FA Cup. They made it to the quarter-final where, unbelievably, they were again drawn to play Arsenal. The tie was to be played at Highbury.

London Albion didn't fancy their chances. Not so much because of the result in the Coca-Cola Cup semi-final, but because of the obvious in-fighting that was going on lately between John Warner and Ted Brinsley. According to the newspaper, if London Albion lost to Arsenal, Ted Brinsley was prepared to sell Mel Thorpe and Dwight Crawford. Unbelievably, Mel would be on his way to Arsenal, Dwight to Blackburn Rovers.

Worse, it was common knowledge that Ted Brinsley's financial problems with the real estate venture were partly the reason for the transfers. Of course the money from the transfers would go into London Albion's funds; there would be nothing shady about that end of the deal. The money was badly needed. Because of the Taylor Report on ground safety, an all-seater stand behind the Clock-End goal at Brompton had to be built; the work was due to begin during the off-season. The tragedy was that if Ted Brinsley hadn't been involved in trying to keep his new company solvent, there would have been no need to sell players; he would have had the money for London Albion (and written if off against tax). London Albion's football fortunes were about to bear the brunt of Ted Brinsley's business dealings.

The fans were disgusted when they got wind of the prospective transfers. But their upset was nothing compared to John Warner's. He and Ted Brinsley clashed about fifteen minutes before kick-off time outside the visitors' dressing-room at Highbury.

'Money can't buy players of that quality. Sell them and we'll be nowhere next year.'

'Lose this cup-tie to Arsenal and our season is over. We're only a middle of the table team, out of everything. We need the money to go towards the new stand. The transfer deadline is only days away, the twenty-sixth of March. The money on offer is good. Now is the time to sell.'

'Sorry, Ted, I don't see things that way. Sell if you like but count me out.'

'What do you mean, "count me out"?'

'I'm off next season. You can hand the manager's job to Sam Gregson.'

Ted Brinsley didn't bother replying. He gave a short glare, turned and made his way along the passageway, up the steps towards the Directors' Box. Lose the match and he'd sell the players – maybe even sell Gavin Byrne the following season if the financial side of things wasn't balancing out. He felt bad about losing John Warner though. But maybe he was going to lose him anyway. Ted wasn't entirely ignorant of the fact that Liverpool AFC would be only too appreciative of John Warner's services.

Professional soccer was a vicious circle, more so off the pitch than on it.

Be a big-time football director? Not on your life!

Reaction came not only from London Albion. As soon as the Arsenal fans caught a glimpse of Ted they got into a slagging routine:

'No League...'

'No Cup...'

'Flog the team, Ted.'

Too many Arsenal supporters read the *Financial Times*

for Ted's liking. They all knew about his business difficulties. It wasn't easy putting up with the taunts. But not giving in, not letting it show, was part of the game.

Ted Brinsley was just getting over the taunts of the Arsenal fans when, after only nine minutes, Dwight flashed the ball to the back of the net off a left-footed drive. The goal stunned the Arsenal faithful and Ted Brinsley's exploits as recorded in the *Financial Times* were quickly forgotten. Arsenal hadn't much time for Albion, and to be a goal down to their bitter rivals, especially in a Cup-tie, was tantamount to disaster. Still, it could have been worse. Instead the goal could have come with nine minutes to go; then there would have been little or no time to remedy the deficit.

Gradually Arsenal raised the pace of the game. Scotch Pete foiled an almost certain goal when he dispossessed an Arsenal striker on the edge of the penalty-area. Then the Albion 'keeper parried a shot wide of the post. Albion were being swamped. Just before half-time Arsenal clawed back the equalizer when, off a well-rehearsed free kick, the ball was sent curling over the Albion defensive wall into the back of the net.

In the second half, London Albion came more into the picture. Scotch Pete led from the back, cajoling his midfield into stepping up their workrate. Arsenal weren't getting the same latitude as in the first half. Mick Bates and Mel Thorpe were getting to the ball first and setting up some great openings for Dwight Crawford and Gavin to run on to. In fact, Gavin was beginning to send the jitters through the Arsenal defence. He scavenged a loose ball inside his own half, made space and laid the ball off. He darted in behind the Gunners' right-full. A return ball was chipped over the full-back's head. Gavin brought the ball quickly under control. He veered in-field, beat two defenders; and, wham! from twenty yards the ball flashed past the Arsenal goalkeeper, jarred off the angle of the upright, rebounded and struck the goalkeeper in the back.

137

Gavin was in like a light and side-footed the ball towards the net, only for it to be cleared off the line.

Albion scored a second goal ten minutes later. Dwight Crawford – again. He powered through the midfield. Played a quick one-two with Craig Shortall and from all of twenty yards rifled a shot past the Arsenal goalkeeper. 1–2.

Arsenal heads were down, but they fought back. They stemmed the tide and for the last fifteen minutes they had Albion under severe pressure. Somehow the 'Albinos' were managing to hold out until, with five minutes to go, Arsenal scored an equalizer off a direct free kick.

Then in the final few seconds…

'Time's up ref!' roared Scotch Pete. 'Ref, what's wrong? You've played over the time.'

The ball was thumped into the London Albion goal-mouth in the hope that an Arsenal boot would connect. Luckily London Albion scrambled it clear.

The ball was thumped in again.

The 'keeper tipped it over for a corner.

The ball came over. The 'keeper mistimed his jump. Scotch Pete headed it wide for another corner.

The ball was played short. Then back to the player who took the corner. He sent the ball across – a curving, dangerous inswinger. An Arsenal head got a flick to it. The ball soared out of the 'keeper's reach into the net.

The referee blew for full time. London Albion were out of the FA Cup.

'He went way over the time,' cursed Mick Bates.

'Easy on, lad, there's always next year.'

Easy on? Always next year? There was always next year for the losers. Some consolation!

Back in the dressing-rooms the Albion players were disgruntled. To lose to Arsenal was a sickener. Worse, they had done themselves proud – only for the referee to rob them by playing well over the time. That was the real sickener.

They sat for at least half-an-hour in the dressing-room, completely dumbfounded. John Warner did his best to cheer them up.

'Always next year,' he echoed.

'Next year?' groaned Scotch Pete. 'Accordin' to the grapevine you won't be here next year. An', boss, what about Mel and Dwight?'

John Warner didn't answer. But the players all knew. Mel and Dwight were on their way out.

The transfer deadline was the following Thursday evening. The fee involved was rumoured to be five million upwards for the two of them. Ted Brinsley would be a fool to turn it down.

The fact didn't do much to cheer up Scotch Pete. The way his knee felt he didn't think he'd be around for next season. It had been acting up a lot lately. As of that moment he didn't feel too good about his future footballing prospects. But, like the true professional he was, he kept his feelings to himself.

Out of the Cup. What was left? Nine or ten Premiership games? Maybe a say in which club would win the Premiership title. But to all intents and purposes the season was over for London Albion.

John Warner and Sam Gregson had a meeting at a central hotel with Ted Brinsley and the other London Albion directors. There was some hard talking to be done. Some stark facts to spell out. It definitely wouldn't be a meeting for the faint-hearted.

A number of sticky issues were finally resolved.

End of season, John Warner would be leaving the club; Liverpool would get their man. Sam Gregson was to take over as manager of the first team. First, he wanted assurance that Gavin wouldn't be sold. Most of the directors were behind him on that particular issue. But the one whose opinion mattered most, Ted Brinsley, was hesitant. Finally he agreed. No matter what – Gavin wouldn't be sold. At least, not for the foreseeable future.

Sam Gregson wanted a substantial increase in wages to augment his promotion to first-team manager. That was agreed. What with the new stand, and all the rest, the Inland Revenue wouldn't get much tax return from the club for the next few years.

Hopefully it wouldn't be long before the London Albion bandwagon would be back on the winning trail. Next season, a Premiership or Cup win. Who was to know?

Next season.

Que sera, sera.

Jake rang Elaine at her apartment in Turin one night in the middle of April. She could hear the dimly muffled sound of music in the background. Seemingly Jake was taking a break during a gig. He was in great form. He was ringing from Birmingham.

'We're gettin' out and about. We're up here all week. They have us in this club. Can't wait to get back to London. I never saw a place so rough. Rows most nights. The bouncers here have door-knockers for ears. They say it's one of the places to be, though. Talk about music soothin' the savage breast. There's plenty of savages in this place. There must be somethin' wrong with our music. I can't see any soothin' goin' on. Some of the clientele'll have the place turned into sawdust before they're finished.'

'Sounds gruesome.'

'It's not that bad, Elaine. The punters love us. The place is packed every night. The record company is really pleased. They're goin' to put out the few pluggers for us.'

'Pluggers, what's that?'

'Pluggers are people who buy air-time for new records. Only in our case the pluggers are goin' to do a huge promotion on us, connected to the club scene. With that kind of publicity we can't go wrong. They're goin' to do an image-job on us. Elaine, you won't know us the next time you see me and Dave.'

'Any chance of making a record?'

'Every chance. It's part of the package. It'll be one of our own numbers. We'll be doin' it around September. Things couldn't be goin' better, Elaine… We have Luke up here with us.'

'Luke's with you?'

'Yeah. He came over two weeks ago. He's on the company payroll.'

'How's he fitting in?'

'Great. He loves it. Loves the travellin' end of things, goin' to different places an' all that. Pity he's not still at school. It'd do his geography a power of good.'

'No problems?'

'Absolutely not. He's happy. All the lads like him. He'll make a good roadie. How's it goin' with yourself, Elaine?'

'Not bad.'

'How's the knee comin' on?'

'Slowly but surely. It'll be all right. Don't forget to keep in touch. Look after Luke.'

'Look after him? He better look after me… I'd better go, Elaine. Some geezer's in the passageway tryin' to flog me guitar.'

'You're not serious?'

'Course I am. Birmingham ain't Birmingham for nothin'.

'See you.'

'See you.'

Elaine hung up. Sat back and watched TV.

Luke was fine. At least that was one worry less. Jake was going to cut a record. Great news. That is if he could be believed. Jake was a great one to embroider the facts, so it was hard to tell. He wouldn't lie about Luke, though. Luke was well, that was a certainty. The more she thought about Jake the more she realised he was cut out for the pop-scene. He was an absolute chancer. He had the nerve to get up to anything. More luck to him!

Elaine's programme was back as planned. The specialist in Brussels had sorted out the soreness and stiffness in her knee and she was now doing light training. There was a long tortuous road ahead, both in the gym and training pitch. She wouldn't get to kick a ball until September, and it would be almost Christmas before she would be risked in an actual game. Only then would they know if the operation had been a success and whether her knee would bear up to the rigours of professional football.

The alternative didn't bear thinking about. She put the though to the back of her mind. Maybe if she had concentrated on athletics instead of football the injury would never have happened.

Maybe.

There wasn't much she could do now. Just try not to think about it and, as Jake would say, go easy on the TV snacks.

13

Although there was still a little over a month to go in the Dublin Schoolboys league, Lar Holmes was convinced Shamrock Boys had the 'D' section wrapped up. He was so convinced that he actually got on the phone to the League about the presentation of trophies.

'Your presentation dinner?'

'What about it?'

'Well, sometimes you have some music before you give out the awards.'

'So what?'

'Well, there's this kid, Jake, used to give me a hand with the team He's gone professional now with a new band. I could ask him to bring the old band into the presentation and play a few songs.'

'I don't think that'd be on.'

'These lads are good. It was rough the way they broke up, they're good. They'd do the presentation dinner for nothin'.'

'I don't think that'd come into it. I'd have to ask the committee. What's the band's name?'

'Scorpion Jack.'

The committee man brought Lar's suggestion up at a committee meeting.

'Never heard of them. Where are they from?'

'Greystones, I think. Sorry, Bray and Greystones.'

'Bray and Greystones… What's the presentation goin' to be? A Macra na Feirme reunion dance?'

'Never mind. Maybe we'll have them.'

'Maybe…'

'They're for free.'

'We'll have them.'

One day in mid-April Gavin came home after first-team training. He had news.

'Hammer, there's talk goin' around about Scotch Pete.'

Hammer said nothing

'He might have to give up playin'.'

'Why?'

'They say he's got some kind of serious injury. Know what that means?'

'No, not really.'

'It could bring you into the frame. Give you a better chance of a renewal contract. A better chance of gettin' into the first-team squad.'

'Bit rough on Scotch Pete, though.'

'Yeah, it's rough. But it could give you your chance.'

Gavin didn't mean to sound callous. At the back of it all he felt sorry for Scotch Pete. All the first-team squad felt sorry for him.

Scotch Pete had never had a job or a trade. It had always been football, football, football. London Albion had looked after him, ever since he had come down from Scotland as a seven-year-old, when his father had migrated in search of work. He had always been around the club as a fan seeking autographs, waiting for a word of advice from the players: how he could improve his shot, how he could go about getting a trial with the club when he was old enough. He would wait outside the players' entrance, ask to carry their kit-bags into the stadium. A legendary half-back with the club, Pete Sinclair, used to hand over his kit-bag to the child – that way he got in for nothing. Funny, that was the custom in the old days; it wouldn't be tolerated now. The players gave the kid a nickname, Scotch Pete, on account of carrying Pete Sinclair's kit. The name stuck, even when the kid grew up to play professional football for London Albion.

Scotch Pete joined the club at thirteen, on an associated schoolboy form, made his First Division debut at eighteen, was selected for Scotland at twenty, played in two

FA Cup Finals and two World Cups. Football had been good to him. He was a household name – a hero.

'I hope Scotch Pete's okay,' said Hammer. 'I hope the injury works out. That it's only a scare.'

'Hammer, it's been goin' on all season. John Warner sent him to a specialist. Nobody'll say what it is though. But it can't be good.'

'Maybe if he rested – didn't play for a while.'

'It's more serious than that. They're sendin' him to another specialist to get a second opinion. The whole thing'll be out in the open in a few days.'

'How does Scotch Pete feel about it all?'

'Terrible. Football's all he ever had. He's never known nothin' else. No trade, no nothin'.'

'Couldn't he go into coachin'?'

'Don't think so. He loved this club. They say when he was a kid he used to go around at half-time spottin' for newspapers in fans' overcoats. He'd ask if they were finished with them. Then he'd smooth them out, make them presentable and go around the pubs sellin' them. Brompton was his whole life. He grew up around here.'

'Hope it works out for him.'

'Yeah, me too.'

The unthinkable happened. Scotch Pete was finally diagnosed as having a flaking of the bone in his knee. He would have to give up playing football, he would have to retire.

The news came as a bombshell to him. He was devastated. It was agreed that he would finish out the season – there were only three matches left – and they would give him a benefit match. A benefit match? He wanted to play football! He wanted to carry on doing the only thing he was good at, the only thing he was capable of doing with competence. Now he would have to give up. Three matches and that would be it. In two weeks' time his life would be over. The impressive mantle of

Scotch Pete, world-class footballer, would be snatched from him.

The club had always looked after him. They had handled his money for him, made all the decisions that mattered. Now he would have to act on his own. He knew he just wasn't capable of doing so – not sensibly. He could sense the future

'See him, know who he is?'

'No.'

'That used to be Scotch Pete.'

'You don't say?'

'Now he's only a bum.'

Scotch Pete began to feel sorry for himself and was soon hitting the bottle.

He played in two of the last three matches of the season. The last match he didn't show up at all. The game was at home, against Norwich, and as usual it was a three-o'clock kick-off. At twenty-to-three, when Scotch Pete hadn't appeared in the dressing-room, the players and backroom staff knew he wasn't going to make it. The game was due to kick-off without him.

John Warner was furious. The dressing-room was in turmoil. They hadn't got a suitable substitute listed among the subs to take Scotch Pete's place. The only solution was to rush in Hammer or Cyril Stevens, that was if they were present in the stadium. Whatever about Cyril Stevens, Gavin knew Hammer was at the match. A message was put out over the Tannoy system requesting Hammer to report to the home dressing-room. He wasn't long getting there. He was handed a jersey and told he was playing centre-half. Before he had time to feel nervous or uptight he was out on the pitch, handling Norwich's attack like a veteran. London Albion won 2–0 and Hammer impressed enough to suggest that he was well capable of handling Premiership football. He would definitely be a candidate for first-team football the following season.

As for Scotch Pete, he *was* playing football at three o'clock. Elsewhere though. Come two o'clock he was in a pub just around the corner from the tenement where he had grown up. He left the pub at five-to-three and went into the yard of the tenement. There were a few kids there playing football. He joined in and kept the game going until 4.45. He had played his last game of soccer.

Scotch Pete never played in his benefit. In fact he never got a benefit. As a consequence of failing to show up for the last match of the season, the men who smoked fat cigars and drank expensive brandy refused to give him one.

It was a very sad story and as Gavin and Hammer watched it unfold they thought back to the day a few years previously when, in Bray Park, a scruffily dressed man approached them and told them they had what it would take to make an impression in the world of football. They wondered if the poor man had travelled the same road as Scotch Pete, the road where heroes can turn into bums, but where the bandwagon and the hangers-on go on and on, forever.

In the end Scotch Pete's bad luck left the door open for Hammer. He was retained and offered a three-year contract on much improved terms. Already John Warner, or should it be said Sam Gregson, was thinking of using Hammer as a straight replacement for Scotch Pete.

There was definitely truth in the saying: 'One person's misfortune can be another's good luck.'

Ask Hammer, who was about to reap the benefits of Scotch Pete's bad luck.

Tough game.

Tough life.

Tough luck.

By mid-May Riverside and Shamrock Boys finished their League campaigns. As expected, Shamrock Boys won the

'D' section of the Dublin & District Schoolboys League. Riverside had come with a late surge and were within sight of promotion. If they won their last match against St Malachy's they would force a play-off with Lourdes Celtic for a place in the 'A' section. The game was a home fixture in the Peoples' Park. Unfortunately, half the Riverside players didn't show up and Mr Glynn was forced into playing a few kids who were hanging about the area. Riverside got beaten 0–3 and lost out on a promotion place to Lourdes Celtic.

Mr Glynn and Harry Hennessy were furious. They felt badly let down. After all the hard work they put in during the year it was a huge disappointment that so many players didn't show up for such a big match. They both felt like throwing in the towel and chucking the team in. But just in case there had been a misunderstanding they went looking for the absent players to see what excuse they had to offer.

'Mr Glynn, we jus' didn't bother goin'. We'd only get walloped in the 'A' section, Most teams don't stand a chance in the 'A' section.'

'But you'll be pushing for the 'A' section again next year. Are you going to start not showing up for matches then as well?'

'Don't know, Mr Glynn. But that 'A' section's too tough.'

'There's no point in having a team if you're not going to aspire to 'A' section football.'

'What does "aspire" mean, Mr Glynn?'

'Nothing you want to know about. Listen, you'll be shoving for the 'A' section again next year, Are you going to put in the effort or not?'

'We'll try, Mr Glynn, but we're not goin' into any 'A'section to get walloped.'

'You won't get walloped. You're good enough.'

'Sure, Mr Glynn. But not good enough for the likes of Home Farm. They've got the pick of Dublin.'

'Well, if you're not prepared to play in the 'A' section there's no point in having a team next year. What are you going to do it I do away with the team?'

'I'll go fishin'.'

'I'll go nothin'.'

Mr Glynn felt totally exasperated. 'That's it then. No team next year. I'll go back down to U-12s and start back up again.'

'Mr Glynn, we'll play U-12s for you.'

'You can't. You're too old.'

'Does that matter?'

'Yes, it does.'

The writing was on the wall. The unruly camaraderie that was Riverside's U-14s was obliterated for all time. Those who wanted to continue with their football careers could either join St Joseph's, Sallynoggin, Shankill, or do the unthinkable: sign up with the enemy, Shamrock Boys.

Mr Glynn was heartbroken. He simply loved the kids. To console him, Harry Hennessy took him to the Dargle Tavern. The longer the evening went on the more sentimental it became. Eventually, Mr Glynn took out pen and paper and placed it on the bar counter. He drew up a list of Riverside's U-14 panel in block capitals and underneath wrote:

> The above players may negotiate their football-ing futures elsewhere. As of now Riverside Boys U-14 are defunct (done away with).
>
> Signed,
George Glynn.

On the way home he went into the corner shop where he knew most of the Riverside players bought their sweets and cigarettes. He got the shopkeeper to display the notice in the front window.

He walked outside, took one last look at the names on

the notice. They reminded him of an unwritten obituary.

He nodded to the shopkeeper, got into his car and drove off.

Early in June Mr Glynn and Harry Hennessy travelled into Dublin for an important League meeting. Well, that was what the League secretary said: 'Be there, it's important. We want every club in the League to be represented.' That meant Lar Holmes would also be in attendance. When it became obvious that Shamrock Boys were going to win the 'D' section Lar had shown up at every meeting; before this he had never gone. And now that his team had won the League he would be there all right, travelling in on the 84 bus, wearing his black County Council donkey-jacket more than likely. He would be all smiles, but without a word to say to Mr Glynn or Harry Hennessy.

On the way to the meeting Harry Hennessy never once shut up. He was intensely knowledgeable when it came to matters associated with soccer. He liked to tell stories about famous players and what they got up to in the distant past.

Mr Glynn got in the odd word. 'You've followed Man Utd a long time, Harry.'

'Yeah, right from the start. I lived there as a kid. Not the same place now, though. There were two Bray men over there around that time: Tommy Hamilton and Spanky McFarlane. Never made it though. Liam Whelan was my favourite. Then after the crash, Ernie Taylor. Little Ernie Taylor was class.'

'Brings it all back, Harry?'

'Yeah, brings it all back. Nothin's the same any more. Never will be.'

And nothing was the same. Not even the Dublin Schoolboys meeting.

The chairman addressed a packed hall: 'You should all know by now why you've been called in tonight. In three weeks time the SFAI are having their AGM in Dublin. They'll be coming by bus, train, maybe even by bike. They'll be coming from all over the country to vote their men on to the SFAI committee. We don't want that. We want us – we want Dubs on the committee. We want each and every one of our clubs represented at the AGM to vote our officials on to the Irish Schoolboys committee so that our players get a fair crack at being selected for the Irish Schoolboys team. We don't want to be dictated to by a crowd from the country, do we?'

The chairman paused, cocked an ear for the expected response.

When it came it reverberated through the hall in a collective grunt. Deciphered it meant: no, we don't want a crowd of culchies running the show.

The chairman concluded: 'Be there. 'Cause they'll be there. And we don't want them there.'

Down in the body of the hall Mr Glynn and Harry Hennessy felt uncomfortable. Possibly Lar Holmes as well, wherever he was among the thronged gathering. They felt as if those nearest would point them out: 'Look, there's a few culchies over here.'

As soon as the meeting was over they drove straight out of Dublin and crossed the border into County Wicklow. Their thoughts were on the future. They had a new U-12 team to groom. A new set of schoolboy tearaways to plague the Dublin Schoolboys League with.

Riverside! Riverside!

Culchies?

Never!

The member of the FAI hierarchy who had told Gavin he might very well make the next European Championship panel had not been wrong. Gavin was called into the full International squad for a qualifier against Austria in Vienna on the sixth of June, a Wednesday. The Irish team manager phoned his congratulations. Most of the players

151

met in Dublin on the Sunday and flew out to Vienna on Monday morning. They had a practice session in the afternoon, followed by a work-out and tactical talk on Tuesday. Tuesday night they had a kick-about in the actual stadium where the game was to be played.

The local papers were full of a past encounter between Austria and Ireland. One article mentioned a 'Butcher of Vienna', because of the player's robustness during the course of the match. The Irish players got a laugh out of that one. A better laugh when they realized that the reference was to an Irish player. They wanted to see the article for themselves, so that they could find out the unfortunate player's name, but the Irish team manager pulled the newspaper away from them and had it removed from the room. He didn't want any slagging to start up when the players got home, as there was a possibility some of them could know the maligned ex-international who had been dubbed 'the Butcher' by the Austrian press.

'What's his name, boss?'

'I'm not tellin', except to say he was a centre-half and played for Millwall.'

'Wasn't Mick McCarthy, was it?'

'Naw, it was well before his time.'

'Eamon Dunphy played for Millwall, didn't he?'

'So what?'

'Well, if this Butcher fella was any good he should've flattened Dunphy in a practice match. It would've saved people a lot of bother. You included.'

So much for the Butcher of Vienna.

The match against Austria proved to be something of a disaster. Ireland lost 1–0. They had come expecting, and needing, a draw. Gavin didn't get a start. He was included in the subs, but never got on to the pitch.

The team had been selected with the emphasis on defence. They had gone a goal down just before half-time. The manager never altered the tactics for the second half.

He hung on with the same defensive formation, hoping to score a goal on the break. But the goal never came. In the last fifteen minutes he made a substitution: he brought on an extra attacker. But the attacker wasn't Gavin. Instead he brought on an old and trusted player, who, for the past two seasons had been on the decline.

Next day the Irish papers were furious. In their opinion, Gavin was the player who should have been brought on.

Gavin, one of the best prospects in the whole English League, developing into one of the top goalscorers ever seen in the League. Gavin should have been brought on, but wasn't. No wonder they lost. The papers were in an uproar.

Gavin took it all calmly. He went back home and said nothing. There was always the next time: a match in September against Spain at Lansdowne Road.

There was always some other day. He was young, he could wait. He knew he had a full future ahead of him.

Epilogue

A crowd was moving in off the main road down by the Dodder. That was on the Ballsbridge side. Head-on from the city centre the approaches were the same. The Ringsend and Sandymount sides were a mass of green and white, chanting and buzzing with football talk. Coming in from Bray, Blackrock and the southside in general, there were lines of cars, as there were on all northside approaches. The Dart trains were shuttling into Lansdown Road station at five minute intervals.

It was match day: Ireland v Spain, a Group Two European Championship qualifying match. Ireland hadn't much to write home about regarding fixtures against Spain, except maybe a 1-all World Cup draw in Seville, and a famous 1–0 World Cup win years earlier in Dalymount Park.

On that occasion the Spanish goalkeeper had punched a cross into his own net. He had panicked under pressure from the Irish centre-forward, Noel Cantwell, a converted full-back. The centre-forward had put him under a lot of pressure during the game. He was expecting the centre-forward to come charging in as usual on one of his characteristic mad-bull charges (in those days you could shoulder a goalkeeper). But the centre-forward never came charging in. The ball swung across from the left, the St Peter's school end. The goalkeeper was half-watching for the ball coming across, half-watching for the centre-forward. The ball swung into the penalty area, right beneath the crossbar. The goalkeeper panicked and instead of catching the ball punched it into his own net. The centre-forward turned and smiled. He had been nowhere near the goalkeeper. He ran back to the centre-

circle waiting for the ball to be recentred. Ireland won 1–0.
   Some of the players:

> Alan Kelly
> Andy McEvoy
> Mick McGrath
> Joe Haverty
> Noel Cantwell
> Tony Dunne
> Charlie Hurley

   Charlie Hurley? What could one say about Charlie Hurley? He was the greatest!
   Another memory: an England goal in the last few seconds that dumped Ireland out of an earlier World Cup. Yes, Dalymount had its memories – when victory was a tackle, the comics in the crowd, the first sighting of a new talent, maybe the surprise of beating a top team in a friendly, but never qualifying for the final stages of an international tournament. Memories and tears. And Dalymount also had its heroes, both on and off the pitch.
   But that was a different time, a different age; now it was Ireland v Spain in a European Championship qualifier.
   Jake and Luke stood just inside the railings of the Berkeley Court Hotel. Jake glanced at his watch and wished Hammer and Elaine would hurry. Only for the fact that he had their tickets he would have gone in and met them inside. Jake was wearing a pair of lensless glasses and an Ireland cap, the glasses as a sort of disguise so that he wouldn't be pestered for autographs. As it was, nobody recognized him in the rush to get to the game.
   Jake and Luke weren't the only ones waiting to get into the Lansdowne Road grounds. Lar Holmes had hired a bus and, full of Shamrock Boys players, it was stuck in traffic about half-a-mile from the pitch. Lar got the bus to pull in, quickly unloaded the kids, and got them to trot along the footpath to Lansdowne Road in double-quick

time. They made it with five minutes to spare.

Mr Glynn and Harry Hennessy were also on their way from Bray, minus their recently defunct U-14 team. But that didn't prevent some of the lads going to the match. They were on their way in from Bray on the Dart, with a life-size cardboard cut-out of Paul McGrath which they had hijacked from a local TV shop on their way to the railway station. They put the cut-out standing in the window of the Dart. One of them put his hand in front of the cardboard image and made rude gestures to all and sundry along the Dart line between Bray and Lansdowne Road.

'Look, Da, it's Paul McGrath.'

Going through the turnstile at Lansdowne Road the operator cracked, 'Got a ticket for him?'

'No. He's goin' on for the last ten minutes.'

Jake, Luke, Hammer and Elaine, now fully recovered from her knee injury, got in with minutes to spare. Best seats in the 'house'. The two teams were already out on the pitch, the press photographers busy all around them. Then they lined up for the National Anthems. Gavin was sixth in the line of Irish players as they faced the tricolour for the Irish Anthem.

Elaine and the three lads felt the emotion of the occasion get to them as they looked down on the pitch. The previous few years flooded their minds in a matter of seconds. Most of all for Hammer. In a way he felt quietly contented. Maybe his contentment was due to the fact that his football career was beginning to progress nicely. That, like Gavin, one day soon it would all happen for him It certainly was a notion which pleased him.

He was quickly brought back to reality; the band stopped playing, the preliminaries were over, the players broke rank and got ready to start the match. A coin was tossed for ends. The teams took up position, and the referee blew the whistle for the start of the match.

At first Luke wasn't overinterested. Two pigeons had

flown in an arc from the top of the stand. He watched them intently, the outline of their wings traced against the grey roof of the stand as they glided to a resting place. An old familiar feeling surged inside him. The pigeon-bug still dug deep. Almost reluctantly, he turned and watched the game.

The first half was even enough, except for the first ten minutes when the Spaniards were very jittery. Ireland had two early chances but didn't make the best of them. This seemed to give the Spanish heart; they settled and gave Ireland quite a few scares with neat ground football. The half ended Nil-all.

At half-time Elaine, Hammer and Jake discussed Ireland's team tactics and Gavin's performance so far. Luke went off to get some burgers. Football tactics? Stuff them! He wasn't interested.

The second half began with the Spanish defending in numbers. They only had one man up front. It was obvious they were intent on holding out for a draw.

A fellow beside Jake said, 'The way you've been talkin' you seem to know that Gavin Byrne.'

'Yeah, we grew up together.'

'Play football together?'

'Yeah, that and all.'

'Were you any good at it?'

'Brilliant!'

Brilliant? What else could Jake say? He couldn't very well tell the truth – that he was hopeless.

Minutes later Gavin connected with a loose ball outside the Spanish penalty-area. He rifled the ball past the helpless goalkeeper. Ireland were 1–0 up.

The crowd went berserk. The roar was deafening. In the stands everyone was standing, punching the air. There was absolute pandemonium in the stadium. The sway of movement was unbelievable – a sea of tossing green. Ireland were on their way!

The fellow next to Jake started annoying him again.

'That Gavin Byrne's brilliant. Bleedin' deadly. I'll have to start followin' London Albion instead of United. I want to see more of that Gavin Byrne. He's some player. Jus' see the way he thumped that ball. It was grease lightnin' You musta been some player if you played with Gavin Byrne. Wha' made you give up?'

'I started a band. I'm a pop star. D'you not recognize me?'

'Naw. Never saw you in me life before.'

'I'm Jake Flynn of Tin Knights.'

'Jake Flynn? Tin Knights? Means nothin', mate. Just a blank.'

'Sure?'

'Positive.'

Jake felt deflated. He took cold comfort from the fact that the match programme gave total non-recognition to Gavin's footballing roots. There was nothing about Shamrock Boys. Nothing about Greystones where it all began – the Railway Field. It was all big-time stuff – London Albion. Not a mention of Shamrock Boys. Lar Holmes would have something to say about that! He'd have more than something to say. He'd be quick to raise the issue by phoning the FAI.

After Gavin scored the goal the Spanish changed tactics. They went on the offensive. With ten minutes to go an Irish player broke through the middle. It was Gavin. He had a clear run to goal. The goalkeeper advanced. He timed his advance so that Gavin wouldn't be able to chip the ball over his head into the goal. He even spread himself as best as he could but still Gavin was able to side-foot the ball calmly into the net.

More bedlam. Another surge of green. Another roar from the packed stadium.

Elaine looked to Hammer, Jake to Luke. They were ecstatic. Gavin had raised his hand and pointed a finger towards the sky when he scored the goal. He kept the finger pointed as he ran back towards the centre-circle.

The gesture was just like in the old days when they all played together, when Elaine wore the Shamrock Boys number 7 jersey. That gesture brought back more than emotions. Memories, seemingly forgotten, flooded back, vividly reborn, as soon as Gavin raised a hand in celebration.

And still the crowd roared, only now it was stronger, more jubilant.

Spain tried all the harder to rescue the game. But no matter how much they battled and varied their play the necessary goals wouldn't come.

Two minutes left.

One minute left.

Two minutes into injury-time.

The referee blew his whistle. Full time.

Jake, Luke, Hammer and Elaine sat back in their seats and waited for the crowd to leave the stadium. They were as excited as everyone else. A great win! They went down to the dressing-rooms and were allowed in. They congratulated Gavin. Then the manager came over.

'How're you getting on?' he asked Hammer.

'Fine.'

'We're having a team reception in the Berkeley Court, like to come?'

'No, thanks. I've already arranged to have a quiet drink with my friends.'

'Nice to meet you, Hammer.'

'Glad to meet you.'

'The best of luck. I hope you make the Irish team soon.'

Jake, Luke, Hammer and Elaine left the dressing-room. Gavin went off to the compulsory team reception.

Outside there were only stragglers, litter and unmanned crowd-control barriers. The level-crossing barrier was down. They stood and waited for the train to pass. It came from the city direction, going out towards Bray. It was the Dublin-Rosslare Express. It flashed past. In less than half-an-hour it would be cruising past the

Railway Field in Greystones, the football pitch where Gavin played his first-ever game of football. The barrier lifted. They walked back to where Elaine had parked her father's car. They got in and drove off to some quiet country pub where they could have a drink and talk about old times.

By the time they had finished their drinks the Rosslare Express would have reached its journey's end, the travellers dispersed to their various destinations.

The friends' lives were different now. They were part of the adult world. Their childhood was gone. Gone in a blur.

Like young champions, gone but remembered.